CHAMPAGNE HARVEST

Journalist Laura Kane believes that French artist and Champagne grower Philippe Beaulieu is involved in the disappearance of a local teenager. However, the dynamic artist has a passionate hatred of journalists, so she keeps her profession and her journalistic investigation secret. Despite her concerns, love blossoms among the vineyards and she finds the missing teenager. However, when Philippe discovers her true profession he feels betrayed. Their love seems doomed — and to make matters worse, so does the harvest . . .

ANN CARROLL

CHAMPAGNE HARVEST

Complete and Unabridged

LINFORD
Leicester

First published in Great Britain in 2012

First Linford Edition
published 2013

A catalogue record for this book is available
from the British Library.

ISBN 978–1–4448–1683–9

Published by
F. A. Thorpe (Publishing)
Anstey, Leicestershire

Set by Words & Graphics Ltd.
Anstey, Leicestershire
Printed and bound in Great Britain by
T. J. International Ltd., Padstow, Cornwall

This book is printed on acid-free paper

The Girl in the Painting

Without a doubt, Philippe Beaulieu was as magnificent as the pictures he painted. He stood chatting to his admirers, smiling and flirting with the women who had gathered for this, his latest exhibition. The fact that the Paris studio was crowded with an unhealthy ratio of ten females to every male made Laura wonder if art was really appreciated more by the fairer sex — or whether it was because the artist was the famous Philippe Beaulieu.

She remained in the background, watching him over the shoulders of his adoring fans, well aware that he hadn't just made a name for himself through his paintings. Although they were unarguably brilliant, it was his celebrity lifestyle that had spiralled him into the limelight. The women he was photographed hitting the Paris nightspots with were all incredibly glamorous — models, actresses, B-list celebrities, even the occasional footballer's former wife.

Tonight, for the launch of his exhibition, his guests were in their best attire and Laura wondered how many of the women here were secretly hoping that they could catch his eye — and turn his head.

A silver tray appeared under her nose and a waiter enquired whether she would like a glass of champagne. With a smile, she took the fluted glass that fizzed invitingly, wondering if it was champagne made from Philippe Beaulieu's own vineyard in the Champagne region, or whether he had brought in a cheaper brand for tonight's minions.

Champagne was another string to his bow. His award-winning champagne was stocked by the most exclusive of restaurants and bought by the elite. It was unlikely that you would find a bottle of Champagne de Beaulieu on the supermarket shelves.

She sipped it, loving the sensation of the bubbles, but finding the liquid itself too sharp for her liking. The effect, however, was instantaneous and she felt a sudden light-headedness. No doubt if she managed to get through the entire glass, she would be swaying giddily back to her hotel room later that evening.

She moved towards the open balconied window for some fresh air, still keeping a low profile, keener to observe than be observed.

Beyond the ornate wrought-iron railings, the moon reflected in the Seine's silvery-black waters. A cruise boat festooned with coloured lights slipped by, filling the night with music and laughter, before fading as it moved on.

To her right the awe-inspiring Eiffel Tower stood guard, and that, too, was outlined in neon lights, like a giant beacon for all of Paris to look up to and adore.

Philippe Beaulieu was talking about

one of his paintings now. He spoke in French, his native tongue. His voice was deep, yet had a soft resonance to it — a melodic, mesmerising sound that had no doubt charmed many a young woman in its time. Not her, however. And, deliberately, she strengthened her guard. She wasn't here to fall under his spell. She was here for a completely different reason.

She listened, trying hard to interpret what he was saying. The painting, like many in this latest exhibition, was of a harvest scene, set in a vineyard. This one showed two people, a young man and a woman, laughing as they picked grapes. It was a simple scene, yet a moment in time captured for ever.

Philippe Beaulieu's skill as an artist was faultless — he understood colour and depth, light and shade, and his attention to detail was second to none. And that, Laura reminded herself, was why she was here.

A man with a camera and camera bag over one shoulder weaved his way across the room. He was shadowed by a young woman with a Dictaphone and notebook. The fact that someone else was here working in the same field as her caught Laura's attention.

They were obviously from a newspaper or magazine and she wondered whether they were here to report on Philippe's exhibition or to snap him with another glamorous blonde on his arm. Although, Laura had to concede, tonight he seemed to be unaccompanied.

Taking a stance directly in front of Philippe, the photographer raised his camera. Instantly Philippe's hand went up, shielding his face — a face that had suddenly become hardened with anger.

It didn't need an interpreter to work out what he said to the photographer, who immediately lowered his camera, full of apologies. The reporter moved in, using her charm to apologise for not first asking if they could take his photograph.

'Get it right,' Laura mused under her

breath, knowing only too well that interviews with celebrities, or indeed the general public, all had to be handled with courtesy if you wanted a good result. And this pair certainly hadn't made the right impression. Though she was surprised that Philippe had been so instantly defensive. He was well used to being photographed. Surely it was second nature for him to smile for the cameras. It was another thing he was good at.

But he looked ruffled and ran his fingers through his black hair in a gesture of barely concealed irritation. And if Laura hadn't before noticed the colour of his eyes, she saw now that they were a brilliant steely-blue, deep set, sparkling with an anger that he was struggling to hold in check.

'I will talk to you about my paintings only,' he said in French, but so blatantly clear that even the most novice language student would have understood it.

Quite obviously he was saying that

the only interview he would give would be to talk about his art. Everything else was out of bounds.

The pair seemed relieved to have salvaged something from their evening's work and listened politely, with the journalist holding her recorder towards his exquisitely shaped mouth and the photographer standing with his camera held at his side. Laura noticed his finger was poised over the button — just in case.

She smiled to herself; he wasn't going to miss a trick. If the opportunity arose to get a picture of Philippe Beaulieu taken off guard, perhaps sipping champagne with someone else's wife, he would get it.

If the photo was cropped, taking out all but Philippe and the other person in question, it could put a whole different slant on a situation, particularly if linked with a clever or damning caption.

Laura knew what could be done. She had seen it on her own newspaper. Not that the 'Westgate Evening Standard' was a tabloid that dished the dirt. It was an honest local newspaper, established 70 years ago, which prided itself on bringing the news to the community in a plain and truthful way. She was proud to be one of the journalists employed there.

Philippe Beaulieu's interview turned out to be a talk about his work, which clearly benefited the entire audience, as everyone stopped their idle chatter and listened, captivated by what he had to say — or maybe, Laura thought, they were just hanging on to his every word for the sheer joy of listening to his voice.

It seemed to her to be quite an in-depth interview, with him talking in great detail about the techniques he used to create the various effects.

And while the complicated language had lost Laura due to the speed and the unfamiliar vocabulary, the reporter nodded continually, as if she really understood what he was talking about.

Laura smiled. She had to give the girl her due. If she was intending to write a story for one of the arts magazines, she would have a real exclusive interview under her belt. But if she was hoping for something scandalous, she was out of luck.

Unable to follow what was being said, Laura moved around the gallery. Philippe's new paintings adorned each of the four walls.

The theme of the exhibition was 'Seasons' and each of the large canvasses depicted scenes of the four seasons in all their glory. Every painting included a person or two, or maybe a small gathering of people working on the land, toying with the vines, tending them, nurturing them.

Philippe's skill in capturing the mood of the moment was what made the paintings so alluring, so captivating. You could almost feel the sun that brought the beads of sweat to the young men's faces, or feel the biting frost that carpeted the bare earth in the winter scenes. You could imagine hearing the voices and laughter of the people immortalised on canvas. It was almost as if you knew them.

Laura stood before the painting that had brought her here. It depicted a teenage girl with auburn hair pinned untidily up, stray tendrils falling over her bare shoulders. Her blouse was off the shoulder, like a peasant's blouse, and she was focused on her work of gathering grapes and filling her basket.

Laura stared at the girl in the picture. Philippe Beaulieu was a brilliant painter, his attention to detail was a credit to him. He captured his subjects so well that the viewer really felt that they knew the subject personally — and in this instance, Laura did.

'*Mademoiselle, vous aimez ce tableau?*'

The voice was mellow, rich as velvet and Laura felt the aura and presence of Philippe at her side so strongly that she almost felt he was touching her.

Startled, she shot a glance at him and

saw, to her surprise, that he was standing at least a foot or so away from her, yet his magnetism was like an electric current drawing them together. She struggled against it, inching away, feeling the colour rise in her throat and cheeks.

She was angry with herself for not noticing the interview had ended. Indeed, the photographer and journalist were nowhere to be seen.

His eyes seemed to be spearing straight through her, but when she glanced up at him again, she saw that his attention was focused on the painting — not on her.

'Exquisite,' she said, shielding her face behind her hair. It was shoulder length and she wore it parted to the side, so that when she needed to, it formed a curtain of golden brown behind which she could hide.

'You are English?' There was surprise in his voice — and something else. Some note that Laura couldn't quite equate.

'Yes, yes, I'm English.' She remained looking at the painting, but trying desperately not to look at the tattoo on the girl in the picture's left shoulder — the identifying mark that confirmed her to be seventeen-year-old Lucy Day, who went missing a year ago from Laura's home town. Laura had personally written countless news reports on the mystery.

Even when the story became old news and people had lost interest in where the teenager had gone, Laura had kept the story alive. She felt she owed it to the girl's mother and stepfather, who were frantic.

'I am familiar with England. What part are you from?' Philippe asked as he took a glass of champagne from a passing waiter and shifted his stance to show Laura that she now had his full attention.

She wasn't sure if she was ready for this. There were too many questions to risk ruining the chance of answers by barging straight in.

She had seen how he dealt with the press, and she sensed that if he knew she was a journalist he would shun her without another word — whether he was guilty of any crime or not.

She knew suddenly that there was only one way of playing this if she was to get to the bottom of the Lucy Day mystery. She turned her head, sweeping her long golden hair back from her face and smiled.

'I'm from London.' It was a blatant lie, but at least she knew London well enough to blag her way through any questions.

Had she told the truth and told him she was from Westgate on the east coast, he might have spotted the link, as that was also Lucy Day's home town. And the last thing she wanted was for him to be on his guard.

'Ah, London! I know the city well.' He spoke in English, his eyes exploring her face making her acutely aware that this was a man who had probably looked at some of the most beautiful women in all of France and beyond. She knew that she would be falling far short from his usual expectations. 'Which part of London?'

She took a sip of champagne to give her a second or two to come up with an answer. She thought of her favourite sport.

'Wimbledon.' She had been there twice and knew the stadium and the nearest underground station. She tried to change the subject. 'This is amazing champagne. Is it from your own vineyards?'

He inclined his head, his mouth curving in acknowledgement, even though she hadn't meant it as a compliment.

'Yes, of course. A Cuvée de Prestige — but you don't have to finish it if you don't like it. I can get you a sparkling water if you prefer.'

She almost choked and noticed that he was trying not to laugh at her. Her colour deepened. No doubt he thought her the most dull, unsophisticated woman that existed this side of the Seine.

'No, it's very nice, really.'

'Well, I think so,' he said, gesturing towards the painting with his glass before bringing it back to his lips. 'So, do you like my paintings or, like the champagne, are they also not to your taste?'

Well, Laura thought, there was no fooling him! She would have to tread carefully regarding her questions. Nevertheless, she couldn't help responding with a bright smile.

'I love your paintings.'

'Thank heavens!' he exclaimed, a tinkle of laughter in his voice that caused quite a few heads to turn. 'I imagine you do, or you would not be wasting a beautiful August evening cooped up in here while the whole of Paris lies waiting.'

Laura sensed the eyes of most of the people in the room on her, quite a few looking her up and down and no doubt wondering why she had turned up to an exclusive art launch in a simple strappy sun dress and flat pumps. The truth was, she had no idea how people dressed for such occasions. Besides, it was a sultry evening, and her attire suited the warmth of the night.

She guessed, too, that most of them would be wondering what they were talking about and would be eagerly mentally translating her conversation with Philippe back into their native tongue out of blatant curiosity.

'So, what is it that you love about my work?' he asked her.

'Well, everything really,' she said, trying to put into words the emotions the paintings evoked in her. 'You bring the scene alive. That one . . . ' she said, moving away from the picture of Lucy Day. 'The frost on the ground and the way it's clinging to the bare branches of the vines, I can almost feel the chill through my own skin just looking at that painting.'

He smiled at her, his blue eyes sweeping the contours of her face. He led her back to where they had stood moments before.

'And this painting? I saw you studying it for such a time. What is it about this one that intrigues you so much?' he asked.

Alarm bells clanged in her head and she knew she had to phrase her answer carefully. She thought for a moment before replying.

'I think it's her mood. She's working — we see all the grapes she's already picked and her hand is reaching out for more, but her expression says that her thoughts are far away.' She turned and looked Philippe straight in the eye. 'I wonder what she was thinking about?'

For a second he held her gaze, and for Laura it felt as if time itself was standing still, like the two of them had been captured on canvas, a moment frozen in time.

Then the moment passed. He rubbed his chin thoughtfully and gazed back at the picture.

'Of her lover, maybe.'

'Did she have a lover, do you know? Is she a local girl?' Laura smiled wistfully, as if she was engaging in the fantasy. But, in truth, she was holding her breath, aware that this was a leading question. If she sounded like a reporter trying to track down a missing girl, she had failed.

'I do not know.' He shrugged. 'People turn up for the harvest. Some are local, but others are gypsies or students in need of the wages. Some are tourists wanting to experience a champagne harvest.'

Laura clung on to the wistful look.

'I wonder what she was. Was she French? She doesn't look French.'

He drew his broad shoulders up once more.

'I do not know.'

Laura looked at him in bemused amazement.

'What? You sat there painting her and you didn't even speak to the girl?'

There was the slightest narrowing of his eyes, as if he was having to think on his feet. And then he replied.

'You know, I do remember. She was French, a student from a village near Lille. She was earning some money during her summer vacation.'

Somehow Laura nodded, accepting his explanation without question, as if she hadn't just heard the biggest, fattest lie of all time. She felt quite sick suddenly.

Philippe was lying, covering up something. Lucy Day had gone missing a year ago and somehow ended up in one of his paintings. Where was she now?

She wanted to run, to get away from this overwhelming, overpowering man. But she couldn't. She needed to know what had happened to Lucy Day.

And Philippe Beaulieu had the answers.

A Question Answered

Outside, a police siren wailed. Not an uncommon sound in this turbulent city, but it blotted out what Philippe Beaulieu was saying to her.

'I'm sorry?'

He inclined his head towards her, crowding her senses with tangy fresh scents, no doubt from expensive bottles and sprays, though she had to admit that he smelled wonderful.

'I was apologising for not knowing your name,' he admitted.

'Oh! It's Laura . . . ' She stopped herself from saying Laura Kane. If he was involved with Lucy Day's disappearance, he could easily have been following the press coverage on the story. And her name was linked with all the local news stories. Frantically, she snaffled her elder sister's married name. 'Stevens.'

He bowed his head graciously, took her hand and brought it to his lips.

'*Enchanté*, Laura Stevens.'

Laura was startled by his kiss. His touch was pleasant, his artistic hand was long fingered and elegant, although it did not feel cosseted. It felt like a working man's hand — strong, the skin hardened in places, as if he actually worked on the land when he wasn't painting — although she couldn't believe that. Someone like him would have enough people tending his vines so he could sit back and enjoy the good life.

They were interrupted then by another woman. Laura had seen her mingling with the guests. She looked to be in her early sixties and possessed a look of sheer elegance and confidence that set her apart from all the other women in the room.

She wore an ivory silk cocktail dress topped by a matching jacket embroidered with cord and tiny jewels. Around her throat was a simple pearl necklace.

Matching earrings could be seen beneath thick, black, perfectly styled hair that was streaked with strands of grey that she clearly made no attempt at concealing.

'Excuse me for one moment, Laura,' Philippe murmured, catching the woman's elbow and steering her aside.

Laura moved towards another of his paintings, angling herself so that she could watch him from the corner of her eye. At one point she distinctly saw the older woman flick a startled gaze in her direction before the two parted company.

Philippe turned towards her again, but was headed off by a small band of women who surrounded him with excited chatter. When Laura glanced his way again, he seemed to be regaling them with stories that had them giggling and blushing.

She merged back into the crowd, wandering from painting to painting, looking now to see whether Lucy Day was in the background of any other pictures. She wasn't, which made it all the more amazing that she had ever spotted the missing girl in the first place.

It had been quite by chance. In the weekend supplement of the 'Westgate Evening Standard' there was a regular arts column. The feature's writer, Laura's friend Diane Jenkins, had written about the forthcoming launch of the exhibition of France's best-loved artist. The column included a photograph of one of Philippe's paintings taken from his new catalogue.

Laura had immediately recognised the girl in the painting as the girl she'd been writing about so much for the last year. The breakthrough had her practically leaping across desks to find Diane.

'Diane, have you got the original picture of this painting?' she had begged.

Diane had the art catalogue in her file and the actual image scanned into her computer. At Laura's request, she brought the image up on her screen.

'Zoom in,' Laura instructed.

Diane focused in on the face and then, at Laura's insistence, over to the tattoo on her left shoulder.

'Look at the tattoo. That's her, Lucy Day! That tattoo was unique. See, it's a musical stave with three notes. Quavers, aren't they? Her mother and stepfather described it to me.'

Diane had raised her eyebrows and slowly said, 'I think you'd better tell the boss.'

The boss, editor Dan England, had been sceptical.

'I can see where you're coming from, Laura, and top marks for being so observant, but it could just be coincidence. The tattoo could be a popular one. I'm not up on tattoos, are you?'

'No, but I will be. Give me a couple of hours.'

She had spent the morning visiting the local tattoo parlours, learning that the pattern wasn't in any of their books. But, try as she might, she couldn't find the tattoo artist who had created it.

By the end of the day she had also researched the life and background of artist Philippe Beaulieu, and discovered his flamboyant public lifestyle.

At thirty-five he was still a bachelor — one of Paris's most eligible bachelors was how most of the magazines referred to him. Flicking through a library of images on him, Laura discovered that he was rarely photographed with the same woman twice.

'Can I go over to France and check him out, please?' Laura had begged.

'Sorry, Laura, I don't think that's a good idea at all,' the editor had replied. 'If you really think it's your missing girl, let the police know your thoughts. It's their job to move in. You can do the follow-up story if they find anything.'

She had brooded for days, seriously considering approaching the police team who had worked with her on the initial enquiries last year.

But at the back of her mind she had a niggling feeling that either Lucy Day was happy in Europe and didn't want to be found — so it wasn't her place to set the police on to her. Or maybe something bad had happened to the missing girl, in which case perhaps more subtle enquiries might be a better approach than for the police to barge in and ride roughshod over everything and everyone.

She decided to let the matter drop — or rather, to *appear* to let the matter drop. But she booked a week's holiday, timing it to start the day before the official launch of Philippe Beaulieu's latest art exhibition in Paris. She organised her press invitation on the basis of covering the exhibition on behalf of her colleague, arts writer, Diane Jenkins.

Standing here now, in this exclusive Paris studio, gazing at these beautiful works of art, Laura realised that Diane would have loved all this. But, of course, she wasn't here for art's sake. She was trying to track down a missing girl.

Laura was wondering what her next

move should be when Philippe Beaulieu returned to her side.

'My apologies for deserting you, Laura.'

'It's no problem, Monsieur Beaulieu. I've probably monopolised enough of your time.'

'It is my pleasure,' he said, placing a hand over his heart. 'And I would love you to call me Philippe. May I re-fill your glass with something that is more to your liking?'

'No, honestly, but thank you. I'm actually getting a taste for it now.'

His eyes lingered a little too long on her mouth, as if she had just told a little white lie. It seemed to amuse him.

'So, Laura, are you in Paris on holiday? Or are you working?'

'Just a short break — a culture break,' she came up with suddenly. 'I love art and galleries and museums — and Paris has so many. It's my treat to myself. Something I've been promising myself for years.'

Although it was a bit of a fib, it was partially true. She had often thought of taking a holiday here and visiting the Louvre again. Her only previous visit had been as a thirteen-year-old on a school trip and she hadn't really appreciated it then. Her explanation tied in, too, with her presence here at his exhibition.

'Have you come with friends? A boyfriend, perhaps?' There was a twinkle in Phillipe's eye as he asked.

Her eyes might have given away the fact that boyfriends were the last thing on her mind at the moment.

'No, just me. Not many of my friends share my interest in art. They would prefer Ibiza to this.'

He wrinkled his nose as if the idea was abhorrent to him.

'We are all different. So what do you do when you are working?'

Lord! She might have guessed that was coming and she wasn't prepared for it. She was glad of the champagne, it gave her a moment to come up with something as she took another sip.

'I'm in the retail trade,' she lied,

although she did spend hours shopping. 'I'm a shop assistant in a shoe shop.'

She groaned inwardly. Lie upon lie upon lie. At this rate her nose would outshine Pinocchio's!

He nodded his dark head and took a sip from his own glass.

She took the initiative to try and find out a little more. She had nothing to lose now. He was bound to grow bored with her in a minute and go off to chat to other guests. If she didn't get some answers now, there might not be another opportunity.

'You must be pleased that so many people have shown an interest in your work. Are these people all friends and art lovers, or are some here from your vineyard?'

His steely-blue eyes scanned the room full of people as he considered her question.

'Some are appreciative of art and some are acquaintances, but there is no-one here from my vineyard, no,' he told her.

So that was that line of questioning gone, Laura realised, struggling on.

'So none of your subjects in the paintings are here? If I'd been painted by a famous artist I'd be first through the door for its exhibition!'

He smiled indulgently.

'My subjects, as you put it, are of modest nature, and besides, most did not even know I was painting them. I sketch swiftly, and then paint at leisure in my studio, using my intuition and imagination. So, in fact, what you see may never really have existed.'

She stared at him, deciding that it would be a massive coincidence if he'd painted a girl who looked exactly like Lucy Day and given her a musical-themed tattoo on her shoulder just from his own imagination.

The woman in the ivory silk outfit caught his eye from across the room and beckoned him over. He turned apologetically to Laura.

'Excuse me, Laura, I am wanted. I think my mother wants to take some photographs for our press releases.'

'That's your mother?'

Yes, of course it was, she could see the resemblance now. Both were tall, elegant and dark, although her eyes weren't such a bright steely-blue, they might have been in her younger days, but had paled a little over time. Their features, the strong straight nose and the well-shaped mouth were similar, and the fact that they dressed immaculately.

Philippe's midnight-blue suit was obviously hand-made and looked very expensive, and his shirt, in a contrasting pale blue, was pure silk. There was no tie, and the open-necked effect gave him the casual air of being the host of this event.

Looking from mother to son, Laura was quite surprised that she hadn't instantly seen the similarities. But then, she knew why she hadn't. In her heart, she would never have dreamed that a man like Philippe would want his mother around in his day-to-day life.

Surely that would cramp his style — a style that left a lot to be desired, if the magazines were anything to go by.

It surprised and impressed her to find that, despite all his womanising, he had a good relationship with his mother.

He was halfway across the room when he turned and strode back.

To Laura's surprise he took her hand.

'Come and join us in the photographs, Laura,' he told her firmly.

'No, I can't!' she exclaimed, not just out of embarrassment, but because if they went out with a press release, her real name might somehow come out — and the fact that she was a journalist and had just spun him a pack of whopping great lies.

But his hand was firmly around hers and she had no choice but to trail after him through the crowd. To her relief, he also gathered three or four other people from his guests, so that it was a small crowd standing around one of his paintings. It wasn't, Laura noticed, the painting of Lucy Day.

Philippe's mother pointed a camera at the group and took a variety of shots.

'*Voila! Merci!*' she announced when she had done. Everyone dispersed, smiling broadly at having being photographed with the famous Philippe Beaulieu.

'There, that was not so terrible, I hope?' Philippe remarked, as she went to move away.

'No, I suppose not,' she said, smiling awkwardly. 'Although I'm amazed that you bother with press releases. Judging by the way you dealt with those journalists earlier, I would say you aren't too keen on the press.'

He lowered his head to hers, his lips dangerously close to her ear so that her entire body began to tingle.

'If I told you that I loathe and detest reporters and the paparazzi with a passion, that I think they are the scum of the earth, the lowest of the low, would that surprise you even more?'

Her heart sank.

'Why?' she asked in a tiny voice.

He straightened and gazed way over her head.

'It doesn't matter why. But I choose to give the newspapers my own words rather than allow them to make up their own version. I advertise my exhibitions and even my champagne news and awards through paid-for editorials. It gives them less scope to run a similar news story of their own invention.'

'I see.'

'And who better to trust with providing the true story without embellishing it than my own mother? She is my press officer and my PA.' His eyes sparkled wickedly. 'And she also makes an excellent chocolate and coffee gateau!'

Laura forced herself to smile. But deep down, his damnation of her field of work stung. Under normal circumstances, she would have jumped on her soapbox and pointed out the good that journalists do. That only the minority scandalise everything.

She would have hammered home the fact that most reporters and newspaper photographers work their socks off every day for very little pay so that the truth is told. Not only that, most were as passionate about their profession as he was about his. But under the circumstances, she remained mute.

One or two of the guests were starting to drift away. The first to leave were couples, who probably were the keen art lovers. The many women on their own, who now appeared to have grouped together conspiratorially, seemed in no hurry to leave.

Laura noted, too, that some of his paintings now had little yellow stickers on one corner of their frames, indicating, she guessed, that they had buyers. Laura hadn't even noticed they were priced, but then perhaps they weren't. Perhaps it was a case of if you need to ask the price, you can't afford it!

The painting of Lucy Day also bore a little yellow sticker.

As guests gradually meandered their way to the exit, Philippe was called away to speak with every single one in person, which he did at length with obvious pleasure and considerable gratitude.

Laura wandered back to the painting of Lucy Day. A woman in her mid-forties in a tightly fitting navy belted dress was standing possessively beside the painting, deep in conversation with Philippe's mother. Laura guessed that they were making arrangements for the sale and delivery of the artwork.

Laura bided her time until Madam Beaulieu went over to another couple, who were also staking their claim on their new piece of art. Then Laura wandered closer to the Lucy Day picture.

She smiled at its new owner, hoping the woman could speak English, because her French certainly wasn't good enough for what she had in mind.

'Such a beautiful painting. I think

this is my favourite,' Laura said conversationally. 'I adore the way the girl is lost in her own thoughts, don't you?'

'Oh, yes. That is what struck me, too,' the woman replied in perfect English, albeit with a Parisian accent. 'She looks to be in a dream.'

'I wonder who she is?' Laura added.

'I do not know who she is,' the woman replied, sounding quite surprised. 'The question did not present itself.'

Laura looked at the woman in astonishment, keeping her voice quite low. The last thing she wanted was for Philippe to overhear her.

'Really? If I had just bought this painting for that amount of money, I would want to know everything about it. Surely when it is in your home and your friends admire it, you will need to tell them something. Unless, in France, that sort of thing just does not matter.'

Judging by the woman's expression, Laura had definitely hit a nerve. With a sympathetic smile, she left her to it and wandered across to the far side of the room, where a group of women had collared the wine waiter and were making him blush.

Standing behind them, Laura glimpsed the Lucy Day painting's new owner talking to Madame Beaulieu. It was obvious what she was asking her.

Madame Beaulieu seemed to be providing the answers without batting an eyelid, making Laura wish she'd simply asked her in the first place.

Although, of course, Madam Beaulieu could be palming her off with the same fabricated story of it being a French student in the painting.

Laura timed her casual saunter back towards the woman in the navy dress as Philippe joined the hen party. Laura was about to ask if she'd had any luck, when the woman herself caught her arm.

She looked and sounded delighted.

'I have discovered the background to my painting!' she exclaimed.

'Wonderful!' Laura exclaimed, expecting to hear the same story that Philippe had given her.

'She is an English girl who had run away from home and fallen in love with a French farm boy.' Her hands clasped together in delight. 'The lovers have a tiny cottage near Pierry.'

'Where?' Laura asked, quite dumbstruck.

'Pierry — a village close to Épernay in the Champagne region.' She placed a manicured hand over Laura's forearm. '*Merci beaucoup*, I am so happy to know all this. If you had not suggested finding out, I would never have done so. *Merci*!'

Laura beamed, unbelievably excited to have the name of the village where Lucy Day could be staying.

Tomorrow, she would hire a car, buy a road map, and drive to Pierry.

She prepared to leave and, glancing around the room, she saw that Philippe's mother was talking to another possible buyer and Philippe was the centre of attention with his core of ardent female admirers.

The excitement of her discovery suddenly turned into a hard, painful lump in her throat. Time to go, she told herself. Time to leave the world of Philippe Beaulieu behind — leave him to his adoring fans. But as she walked towards the door, she felt as if she was leaving something behind.

A tiny piece of her heart.

A Dinner Date

Leaving the gallery, Laura stepped out on to the Paris streets. Despite it being a warm evening, she shivered slightly.

Wrapping her arms around herself, she crossed the road to walk alongside the river. Gazing down, the lights from the cruise boats sent myriad dappled colours dancing over the black water.

The evening crowds seemed to be made up of couples. Everyone seemed to be holding hands or walking arm in arm. For a moment she felt wistful, despite the success of having a new lead in tracking down Lucy Day, she felt unaccountably empty.

She was so wrapped up in her work and loving her job, she had never wanted to change that for marriage or settling down with someone, even though one or two of the men she had dated in the past had hinted at planning for the future. But the slightest inclination of having to give up her independence had her running for the hills. Or rather, giving them their marching orders.

But finding herself alone now in this romantic setting made her wonder if maybe life was passing her by.

She rubbed her upper arms, rallying herself to stop letting her emotions run away with themselves. She was happy with her lot. More than happy. She loved her job and had no intention of changing her way of life. She had her own flat in Westgate, a number of good friends, and a varied social life — what more could any girl ask for?

'Laura!'

She heard someone calling her name. Startled, she spun round and saw, to her utter amazement, Philippe running along the pavement towards her, his jacket flying open, and his black hair swept back from his forehead.

Oh, my goodness, he's found me out, she immediately thought. Her second thought was whether or not she would be able to out-run him!

But then she saw that there was a smile on his face, a ridiculously boyish smile that made her heart do an unexpected cartwheel.

'Philippe!' she exclaimed as he came panting to a halt beside her. He rested his hands on his upper thighs, bending double. She stared at him. 'Are you OK?'

He straightened, still smiling, taking in a great lungful of air.

'Yes! Yes, I am good. Perhaps not as fit as I thought I was, but good.'

She waited, confused, as people stepped around them, one or two casting them curious glances, no doubt recognising Philippe.

'Did I forget something?' she asked, anxiously checking she'd still got her bag.

'No — but I did,' he said. 'I forgot something.'

She frowned, but guessed there must have been a token of some kind to mark the exhibition's launch which she'd left without.

'What?'

His fingers swept his hair back, and he looked suddenly incredibly shy. He hesitated.

'I forgot to ask you for your phone number, or where you are staying. And, most importantly, I forgot to ask if you would like to end this evening with supper and a glass of wine with me — not champagne,' he added with a wry smile.

Laura's mouth literally fell open.

'You're asking me out?'

'I would be honoured.'

'Why?' The word was out before she could stop it, because all she could think of were those photographs of him with glamorous women. Even his fan club at the exhibition looked more his type. By comparison, she literally felt a real plain Jane.

A dark shadow passed over his eyes.

'Why would I not? You are a lovely young woman — you said you did not have a boyfriend. You are in Paris unaccompanied. And . . . ' the shyness was back, making Laura catch her breath. 'And I like you. I don't know if you like me, but maybe you will let me know once we have sat down together and got to know each other a little better.'

She was completely dumbfounded, and more than a little flattered.

'I don't know what to say.'

'It is simple. You just say, 'I would love to have supper with you, Philippe'.'

She had the sudden urge to giggle. She looked at him, standing there, one black eyebrow arched, waiting hopefully, his expression that of a little boy, peering through a toy shop window on Christmas Eve. Finally, she did giggle.

'Oh, go on, then!' she said with a laugh.

'Ah, bravo!' he said, taking her hand and threading it through the crook of his arm. 'I am a happy man.'

Slightly breathless and barely believing how things had turned around in the space of a few moments, Laura found herself strolling along, arm in arm with France's most eligible bachelor.

'What do you like to eat, *ma chérie?*' he asked, glancing at her.

Her heart was racing. People were looking at them. She even saw one man with a camera taking a sly snapshot of them both — or at least of Philippe. The man didn't look like a professional photographer, though, she was sure of that.

'I don't have very sophisticated tastes. I've never tasted frogs' legs or escargot, but I'm sure I wouldn't like them,' she said.

He inclined his head closer to hers, so that she felt his breath against her cheek.

'I don't like them, either! But do you eat meat? Do you like steak?'

'Oh, yes, absolutely!' she answered, remembering that all she'd eaten today so far was a ham baguette, and that was hours ago. Her stomach rumbled at the prospect of food.

'We will get a taxi.'

A moment later he had hailed a taxi and they were seated in the back seat en route to their destination, which Laura thought sounded very swish. No longer with her arm through his, she sat demurely with her bag on her lap, suddenly feeling extremely foolish.

She never got into cars with men she didn't know — never. Yet somehow Philippe had her breaking the habit of a lifetime.

Another thought flitted through her head. Could he have picked Lucy Day up as easily? Lucy Day had never been seen again.

To her relief, however, it was just a short journey and the taxi driver pulled up outside a well-lit restaurant with tables that spilled out on to the pavements. Philippe thanked the driver and paid him, and whatever tip he gave, it had the driver beaming from ear to ear and heartily wishing them both a wonderful evening.

Philippe's hand was at her elbow as he steered her inside the restaurant. Immediately the head waiter made a bee-line for them, obviously recognising Philippe. And if he wondered what a famous man-about-town was doing being seen out with a simply dressed plain Jane, there wasn't an inkling of this in his expression.

He was polite, courteous and directed them both to a secluded table that was tucked away behind giant stone plant pots filled with exotic ferns and a crystal and marble fountain.

Leather-bound menus were presented and wine glasses upturned. Philippe spoke to the waiter in French and to Laura in English, switching from one language to the other with effortless expertise.

'What would you like to drink, Laura?'

'I would really love a spritzer, white wine with soda.' She grimaced as Phillipe's eyebrows arched as if she'd just committed a mortal sin. 'I did tell you I didn't have sophisticated tastes.'

'If it is what you like, that is perfect for me.' He explained to the waiter, ordering himself a particular named bottle of Burgundy, which she guessed was a favourite of his, as the waiter nodded expectantly before disappearing to get their drinks.

Laura opened the large menu and gazed down the rows of courses, very few of which she understood. She glanced over the top of her menu to find a pair of blue eyes focused directly on her. For a second she thought his eyes were regarding her with hostility, or maybe it was curiosity, and then he smiled and his face lit up.

'I'm trying to make sure I don't order raw steak.'

He entwined his fingers together, his hands resting on the table, his gaze suddenly quite tender.

'How do you like your steak?'

She grimaced again.

'Well done. I know, I'm a heathen! I can't bear this red in the middle stuff.'

He nodded.

'There we differ, I prefer mine only just seared in the pan. Shall we have dauphinoise potatoes and seasonal vegetables to accompany it? Or they do French fries — chips, if you prefer.'

She coloured slightly, deciding that even she wasn't going to be wined and dined in a posh French restaurant and order chips.

'Dauphinoise potatoes sound lovely.'

'And would you like a starter, soup or paté, maybe?' he went on.

She put down the menu.

'Thank you, but I think the steak will be enough for me. But, please, you go for it.'

He smiled.

'A steak will be perfect.'

The waiter was back just as the wine waiter served their drinks. Philippe waived the offer of tasting his wine, and placed their order.

When they were left in peace again, he raised his glass in a toast. Laura did likewise.

As their glasses came together in a melodious chink, he spoke again.

'I make a toast to honesty. Nothing good can be built on dishonest foundations.'

She felt a tiny muscle spasm around her mouth as she recalled the pack of lies she had spun since meeting him. But then she remembered the big fat lie he'd told her about Lucy Day being a French student.

She raised her glass and met his penetrating gaze with equal intensity.

'To honesty,' she said, knowing sadly that neither of them meant a word of it.

The meal was perfect. Laura couldn't remember when she had ever tasted a steak cooked exactly how she liked it. It was no wonder that Philippe ate regularly at this particular restaurant. Laura couldn't help but wonder, however, just how many different women he had brought here.

While they ate, the conversation was light with Philippe suggesting places of cultural interest that she ought to see while she was in France. He was knowledgeable and interesting and she enjoyed listening to what he was saying, not just because of what he was telling her, but because she found herself liking the sound of his voice. And liking the way he gesticulated with his hands when he was talking about something that he was particularly passionate about, and liking the face and the eyes and the mouth that was there, facing her across the table.

'And what of your interests, Laura?' he asked, setting down his knife and fork, and linking his fingers in that way of his. 'What are you passionate about?'

She almost forgot. She almost said that she was passionate about her work, of researching a subject, understanding it well enough so that she could write it up in a way that the message came across with clarity and simplicity. That she cared about the rights and wrongs of this world, of the suffering of people less fortunate.

And her passion was finding ways to

write about these things so that they might make a difference.

But, of course, she couldn't tell him all that, because she wasn't a journalist — she was a shop assistant, selling shoes. She selected her words with care.

'I care about people and injustice,' she began. 'There is so much unfairness in this world. I care about poverty and the great divide between the haves and the have nots. I care about the war-torn countries and the poor families who are caught up in fights that they have no control over, while the powers that be use them as pawns. I care about cruelty . . . '

'And are these the things you talk about when you are fitting ladies out for new shoes?' he asked blandly, looking at her as if she was talking way above her station.

Was he mocking her? She wasn't sure, but she changed tack immediately.

'No, then we talk about make-up and what's on TV,' she said sarcastically. 'But you did ask me what I am passionate about.'

He reached across the table and touched her hand lightly. It sent tingles through her veins. His expression was intense.

'So why, then, are you selling shoes?' he asked, seeming genuinely interested.

She didn't answer. Instead she reached for her glass.

Although she had enjoyed her spritzer, a little earlier Philippe had coaxed her into trying a small glass of the red wine that he had ordered. It complemented the steak so well that Laura found herself preferring it to her original choice of drink. She sipped it now, feeling her pulse racing much too fast.

'Is the wine to your taste?' he asked, topping up his own glass and holding the bottle over hers. 'Can I offer you a little more wine?'

'Thank you, it's really nice,' Laura said, deciding to bring the conversation back to a more manageable level. 'I had no idea I could enjoy red wine so much. It's always been a bit hit and miss with me.'

'I thought you would like this one,' he said, showing her the label, perhaps so that she could order it herself when she was back home. 'It is very rich and fruity. The ladies do generally like this one.'

Laura raised her eyebrows challengingly.

'I see, so I'm par for the course, am I?'

He looked horrified.

'Absolutely not!'

Her heart sank. Obviously she wasn't in the same league as his glamorous dates. Stupid of her to put herself up on that pedestal. Well, he had shot her down in burning flames in no time. Her appetite vanished.

'Have you had enough to eat?' he asked as she put her knife and fork neatly together on her half-finished plate, an unpleasant dryness in her throat.

'Yes, that was wonderful, thank you,'

she said stiffly, feeling suddenly like he had done her a big favour in buying her a meal, introducing her to the finer things in life. Perhaps he thought she looked in need of a good meal, and she was his good turn for the day.

'Would you like a dessert? They make the most wonderful apple charlotte . . . '

'No, really. I couldn't eat another thing.' She forced a smile.

'A coffee, then?'

She shook her head.

'No, really.'

'You won't mind if I have one?' he asked, his tone sensing that the mood had changed.

'Of course not,' she answered, needing to get away from him for a moment to try and get her thoughts in order. This man was starting to get under her skin. She pushed her chair back to stand up. Immediately he was on his feet, and a waiter was holding her chair for her. Laura looked lamely from one to the other.

'Excuse me.'

Standing in front of the huge gilt-framed mirror in the Ladies' room, Laura realised that her assumption was probably right. She did look in need of a good meal. The strappy sun dress and flat shoe look had seemed right when she set off this morning, but now, surrounded by exquisite furnishings, the wealthy and the elite, she looked like a pauper.

She wore little make-up anyway, but the mascara and lipstick that she had applied hours ago were long gone, and her hair was wild and windswept. She rummaged in her bag for a hairbrush and make-up, to try to repair the damage.

Philippe was sipping black coffee when she finally returned. He stood and the waiter held her chair while she sat down.

'Are you sure you would not like a coffee — or tea, maybe?'

'No, thank you. I really should be getting back.'

'There is someone waiting for you?'

he asked, looking curiously at her.

'No. I'm just a little tired.'

'Ah!' he said, summoning the waiter, speaking quietly to him.

Laura heard him asking for a taxi. She felt suddenly ungrateful. He had done nothing wrong. In fact, he had been the perfect host — attentive, generous. It was crazy that such little comments he had made had affected her so, to have touched a raw nerve so easily.

'Philippe, the meal has been lovely. Thank you so much. I've really enjoyed it. And your company,' she added quickly.

'Ah, yes. As I said earlier, I will discover whether you like me after we have spent a little time together.' He inclined his head to one side, awaiting the verdict. 'Now we have spent some time together, perhaps you will tell me what I would like to know.'

She stared down at the tablecloth, letting her hair fall over one eye, unsure what to say.

'It is too difficult, yes?' he suggested. 'Maybe you wish to spare my feelings. I can take it, I am a man.'

She glanced up to see him chewing his fingernails in terror. She burst out laughing.

'Idiot!'

'That is your verdict?'

'Yes!' she said, still laughing.

'Then we shall go. My heart is broken.'

Laura found herself laughing all the way to the kerb. A taxi was waiting and the doorman was holding the car door open for her. Her laughter faded. Suddenly not wanting this to be the last moment she shared with Philippe, she turned anxiously towards him.

'Philippe, I'm . . . '

'Please, get in,' he said.

She had neither the choice nor the words to say how much she had enjoyed being with him. Nor how desolate she was going to feel once the taxi door was closed and she was on her way back to her hotel. As she sat down on the back seat her heart felt like lead.

What had this man done to her?

Her common sense told her that it was obviously a good thing that she wouldn't be seeing any more of him. Already he had too strong a hold over her emotions. It was good that she was leaving him now, before she got really hurt.

'Goodnight, Philippe,' she murmured, trying to give him a smile and failing.

But to her utter surprise, he slid into the back seat beside her, his thigh pressing against hers. The car door slammed closed and a mixture of relief, excitement and terror swamped her.

Without a glance at Laura, he spoke to the driver, indicating him to drive on.

As the taxi veered out into the night's traffic, Laura found herself trembling — and fearful suddenly that she had just stepped into a dangerous trap.

Pushing all her fanciful emotions to the back of her mind, she had to face facts. Whether he would admit it or not, this man at her side had met Lucy Day — and none of her acquaintances back home had ever seen her again.

Did the same fate await her?

The Champagne Region

They drove in silence for the first few moments with Laura's heart racing, and a million and one thoughts tumbling through her mind. It was one thing laughing and joking with a wealthy man in the safety of a busy restaurant, but being alone with him was something quite different.

She could feel the heat of him against her skin, and his thigh was closely pressed against hers. She could move, inch further away, but that might seem churlish. But to remain so close — wasn't that sending out the wrong message to him?

'Laura,' he said at last.

'Yes?'

'I know I am a man of great insight and some might say a fount of all knowledge, but even I cannot guess which hotel you are staying at.'

She took a sideways glance at him and saw that black eyebrow arched. She felt suddenly quite ridiculous.

'Oh, I thought . . . '

'You thought I was kidnapping you. Absconding with you to take you to my cellars and hold you there at my pleasure?'

She couldn't help but laugh — both at him and at herself.

'It crossed my mind. I wasn't expecting you to come with me.'

'To put you into a taxi would not be so gallant of me,' he said, turning in his seat a little so that he could look directly into her eyes. His arm was resting casually around the back of the seat, not touching her. 'I try always to be the perfect gentleman.'

She had the most fervent wish suddenly for him to drop the gallant act for a moment and put his arm around her. But then she reminded herself that she could in fact be dealing with someone who had possibly committed a crime here. Why else would he lie about Lucy Day?

She met his gaze, looking deep into those steely blue pools to try and see if there was danger lurking there, or whether the only danger came from her losing her heart to him.

'You have beautiful eyes, Laura,' he said, surprising her. 'As green as the sea. I should like to paint you, to try and capture this colour and those tiny flecks of gold that I see shining there. May I?'

She gasped.

'Are you serious? You want to paint me?'

'It would be an honour.' He took her hand, cupping it between both of his like it was a fragile flower. 'And a pleasure.'

She was glad of the darkness of the taxi to hide the colour that suddenly scorched her neck and cheeks.

'I don't know what to say.'

'It is simple. You just say, yes, Philippe, I would like you to paint me.' That glint was back, transforming his gorgeous smile into something even more irresistible.

Laura pulled her hand free from his, and gave him a playful slap.

'You're teasing me, Philippe Beaulieu. You don't want anybody as ordinary as me in your paintings. For one thing, no-one in their right mind would buy it.'

'It would not be for sale.' He captured her hand again and held it tight. 'It would be for me.'

For a moment she didn't know what to say — didn't know what he was saying. Was this his usual chat-up routine? Was this how he lured women into his arms? She didn't know and suddenly felt way out of her depth.

She told him the name of the hotel she was staying at, then drew her hand free from his. She turned her head aside to stare out of the taxi window, her hair falling across her face, shielding herself from his gaze. Philippe leaned forward and spoke to the driver. The man nodded, recognising the name of the hotel, which was just as well, as all coherent thoughts as to its actual address had now vanished from Laura's head like vapour. Philippe was having a very bad effect upon her.

'What are your plans for tomorrow, Laura?'

She forced herself to answer brightly.

'I thought I would hire a car and see some of the countryside.' It was a half-truth, not quite a lie.

He linked his fingers in his lap.

'So you will not be visiting La Louvre tomorrow?'

'Maybe. I haven't really decided.' She met his gaze, calmly looking into his eyes, and pretending they had no effect upon her at all. 'That's the nice thing about holidaying alone. You can just wake up and decide what you want to do without asking anyone else's permission.'

'Ah, yes, I know that so well. But sometimes it would be nice to wake up and want to share your day with someone special.'

'Yes, well, I'm sure that's never been a problem for you.'

She felt rather than saw the frown darkening his eyes. When he spoke he sounded almost offended.

'*Voila*! There, you see why I detest the media. You are judging me, Laura, on what you have read about me, not what you know for yourself.'

She tried to keep her tone light. There was no way she could let her thoughts show. Trying her hardest to make a joke of it, she said, 'There's an old adage that the camera never lies — and I've seen photographs of you, Philippe.'

'Even in England? I thought the English press had their own victims to harass,' he said, sounding quite amazed that his exploits had reached foreign shores.

Laura had to think fast. In truth, the photographs she'd seen of him out and about with models and actresses were from researching on the internet, and all the stories she'd found had come from European magazines. But to admit that meant admitting the fact that she'd been researching him before today — which might just give the game away about her true profession. She was glad when he didn't dwell on it.

'And what you say about the camera never lying, that is the biggest lie of all,' he said, his tone hardening. 'If you only knew what goes on in the world of magazines and media, you would never trust another word that you read.'

'I don't agree, actually,' she argued, not about to let him get away with such a gross generalisation. 'I think it depends on which papers you choose to read. Some are scandalmongers, I agree, but others provide the public with the truth.'

'Ha!' he exclaimed with a mirthless laugh. 'Show me one editor who would not twist a story around if it meant selling more magazines. You only have to look at the headlines to see they are written to shock.'

'Some editors are conscientious, I'm sure.'

'I have yet to meet one.'

The taxi slowed to a halt, and Laura recognised the entrance to her hotel. There was no doorman waiting to open doors for them here.

'Here we are. Thank you,' she murmured, wishing they hadn't ended their journey on such a sour note. 'And thank you for the lovely evening, the exhibition and the meal.'

He made no attempt at moving, and Laura went to exit from her side of the vehicle, but his hand captured hers, holding her back.

'You say that tomorrow you might hire a car and explore the countryside?'

'Yes, or I may look around the museums and galleries of Paris.' She felt as if she were being deliberately awkward, and hated herself for it.

He smiled wistfully.

'Ah, yes, you have only yourself to please. May I make a suggestion?'

'Yes?'

'That your explorations take you here, to this place.' He took a black and gold business card from his pocket and handed it to her. 'The Épernay region is wonderful. It is my home, and I would like you to visit. I would like to paint you, Laura.'

In the darkness of the taxi she could feel the embossed effect on the card, but more than anything she was aware of his fingers against her fingertips as they both held the card, and the fact that his body had turned towards hers, and his lips were so tantalisingly close.

'I'm . . . I'm really flattered, Philippe.'

'And I would be honoured if you said yes.' He brought her hand to his lips, placing the lightest of kisses to the back of her fingers. 'Goodnight, Laura, sleep well.'

'Goodnight, Philippe.'

Releasing her, he was out of the taxi and opening the door for her in an instant. He gallantly took her hand once more to ensure her safely on to the pavement and up the steps to the hotel's glass doors.

'*Bonne nuit, ma chérie.*'

Then he was gone, back in the taxi, his face at the window and his hand raised in a light salute. Laura waved back, then watched as the taxi pulled away, watching it until the tail lights had merged with a hundred others.

She walked through the hotel's small lobby and up the stairs to her room, feeling as if she had just emerged from a dream. Could she really just have been wined and dined by one of France's wealthiest men — maybe even a real bad boy, if her fears over Lucy Day were grounded?

Closing her bedroom door, Laura got ready for bed, still pondering over the question of Lucy Day. The girl had disappeared off the face of the earth after encountering Philippe — whether it was because of him, she still had to find out.

She looked at the business card. It

was her invitation to delve deeper into this mystery, but on the other hand it might also be a calling card to her own demise emotionally. Getting too involved with this man would not be without its dangers, to her heart at least.

Sitting up in her bed, the sash window half down so that the cool evening air fluttered the lace curtains, she continued to study the business card. It was elegant and had the Champagne de Beaulieu motif of a champagne cork entwined with the initials *CB* in one corner. It had everything there; his telephone numbers, his e-mail, his website and his address. She read the address again, and blinked in surprise at the village near Épernay where he lived — Pierry.

The village where Lucy Day was supposed to have moved to with her French lover. So close to Philippe Beaulieu! He would know her! Undoubtedly he would know her. So he had lied. But why?

Turning into her pillow, still clutching his card, Laura told herself that she would get to the bottom of this mystery no matter what.

★   ★   ★

Warm sunlight across her face awoke her. Laura blinked open her eyes and she squinted at her wristwatch to see the time was barely seven o'clock. Instantly her thoughts flew back to last night and Philippe's face was there in her mind as if it had never gone away. Her heart did a little flip.

He was no reason to feel excited, she told herself. Good looks and charm did not necessarily mean he was a decent human being. In fact, the opposite could be true if he did have something to do with Lucy Day's disappearance.

She showered, hoping the stream of warm water would wash away the effect the man had had on her after just a few hours in his company.

Drying her hair, it occurred to her

that she ought to text someone back home, just to let them know she had made contact with Philippe and that she intended driving to Epernay. If she disappeared off the face of the earth, at least someone would know where to start looking.

But that thought, coupled with the memory of Philippe last night as they talked and laughed, just didn't gel together. The man who had been so charming and attentive to her could not possibly have done anything underhand to another person.

But why had he lied?

The thought echoed around her head. He had lied blatantly. Lucy Day was no more an anonymous French student than she was.

Laura got only as far as thinking about texting someone back at work, then changed her mind. She would see what the situation at Pierry was before involving anyone else.

She dressed in a denim skirt and a buttoned sleeveless top and went down to breakfast. There were some small maps in the hotel reception, and she took one through to the restaurant to work out the route from Paris to Épernay, wondering if she would be best to check out of this hotel and find another one in the Champagne region once she got there. Driving back here again tonight seemed quite pointless.

As she tucked into warm croissants and apricot preserve, she decided that was probably her best option. But first she had to hire a car, as it would give her more freedom to explore rather than travelling by train.

On her way back to her room, she informed the receptionist of her intention to check out, and asked if she could recommend a car hire firm nearby.

'I'm going to drive to Épernay,' she said, struggling to find a French interpretation as the young woman looked blankly at her. 'I need a car — *J'ai besoin d'une voiture.*'

The receptionist's face lit up and she

pointed to the main doors.

'*Oui, la voiture attend dehors.*'

If Laura had understood her correctly, she'd said the car was outside, but she guessed she meant there was a car hire firm just outside, but even if there wasn't she could probably find a taxi which could take her to one.

Returning to her room, Laura packed, double checked she hadn't forgotten anything and took her case back downstairs to check out.

The receptionist flashed another warm smile which puzzled Laura, considering she was prematurely checking out rather than checking in.

'*Votre voiture . . .* ' the receptionist said, then in her best English added, 'Eez waiting.'

'You've booked a car for me?' Laura exclaimed, delighted with the service here, and glancing through the glass doors of the hotel, and spotted a car parked just outside, complete with driver.

She wasn't sure if this was a hire car

or a taxi, but decided that it would no doubt become clear once she had spoken to the driver. Thanking the receptionist, Laura wheeled her suitcase out into the morning sunshine.

It wasn't a taxi, that was for sure. It was a plush top-of-the-range limousine and the driver was female, complete with uniform and cap.

It felt ridiculous to have the woman get out of her vehicle and open the passenger door for her, and suddenly Laura realised that this car couldn't possibly be for her.

'I think there's been some mistake. I want to hire a car for a few days. I think the hotel receptionist has phoned you by mistake.'

'Mademoiselle Laura Stevens?'

'Ah! No — ' Laura began to say, then it dawned on her. Only one person could think of calling her by her made-up surname of Stevens. 'Philippe Beaulieu sent you?' she exclaimed in shock.

'*Oui!* You are Mademoiselle Stevens?'

'Well, yes, but — '

'Please.' The chauffeur smiled a perfect smile, while gesturing for her to get into the car. 'Monsieur Beaulieu has requested your company at his home.'

Laura dug in her heels, stunned by the audacity of the man.

'Has he, indeed? A request is one thing, but there's quite some pressure here that I really don't care for.'

The chauffeur glanced at Laura's suitcase.

'But you are moving on to another place, *oui*?'

'Yes, I am, but . . . '

'May I ask where you are going?' Her English was perfect — only the accent proclaimed that she had been born and bred in this country.

'Épernay, actually.'

The chauffeur smiled, raised her eyebrows and indicated the empty front passenger seat.

Still Laura refused to budge.

'I prefer to have my own transport. I

intend to see some of the countryside at my own pace.'

'Of course,' she replied. 'My understanding is that Monsieur Beaulieu's time is limited, which is why he hoped for you to come today. I will personally arrange for you to have your own car once I have taken you to his home.'

Laura heaved a sigh of relief, realising that this wasn't too bad a situation — a free ride to the Champagne region and the opportunity to question Philippe discreetly at length.

Not for a second did she allow herself to feel even the slightest bit excited at having him send a car for her — and that it had been waiting quite some time, although there was no denying that deep down in her heart there was a tiny quiver that wouldn't be stilled.

'OK, you win. I'd be pretty stupid to turn down a free lift,' Laura said, knowing she sounded ungrateful, but not wanting to be beholden to anybody. 'Shall I put my case in the boot?'

'Allow me,' the chauffeur said, taking it from her.

Laura slid into the passenger seat, glancing around the vehicle for signs linking it to Philippe. She didn't know what exactly, but there was nothing to personalise the car. It was simply clean, comfortable and luxurious.

Happily, the chauffeur was also an excellent driver and managed the frantic *périférique* — the city's ring road — with expertise. Once on the main highway heading towards the Champagne region, Laura felt she could chat to her without fear of distracting her from her driving.

'So you're Monsieur Beaulieu's chauffeur?'

'*Oui*, and other duties,' she remarked, not taking her eyes from the road. 'I drive Madam Beaulieu mainly, as she does not drive. I am also employed by the family to show visitors around our vineyards. And occasionally Monsieur Beaulieu needs my services in other ways, too.'

Laura took a sideways glance at her. There was no mistaking the woman was attractive with her blonde hair pinned up beneath her chauffeur's cap and impeccable make-up on a face that could probably have secured her a job as a model had she wished.

'He said he wants to paint me,' Laura remarked, laughing at the ridiculousness of it. But at the same time, not forgetting why she was here in this country. 'We only met last night! Is he always so impulsive?'

'No, I do not think so.' She turned her head and glanced briefly at Laura. 'He must have seen something in you that interests him.'

Laura had the distinct feeling that the chauffeur personally couldn't see anything of interest, and to be honest Laura felt quite dowdy next to her. The woman was tall, slim, blonde and beautiful — the sort of woman Philippe would normally be photographed out on the town with.

They drove on, with Laura making

the most of the conversation, but learning nothing from her discreet questioning about other people who had sat for him in his paintings.

Gradually, as the miles slipped by, the changing landscape told Laura that they were entering the Champagne region. The fields of crops became fields of lush vineyards — row upon row of green vines laden with ripe fruit. Before long the chequered landscape criss-crossed the entire vista for as far as she could see in every direction. Opening her window a little, she could even smell the grapes on the breeze.

'What an amazing view.' Laura sighed. 'The grapes look ready to be harvested.'

'*Oui*, it will be any day now. Another day or two of sunshine and it will begin. I think this is why Monsieur Beaulieu wished for you to come today. Tomorrow or the day after his harvest may begin and he will be too busy.'

'I see. Is it all done by hand?' Laura

asked, gazing in wonder at the thousands of acres lush with fruit as they drove on.

'Ah, *oui*. It is against the law to pick the grapes any other way than by hand,' the chauffeur answered. 'It is not the way.'

'Do the same people return each year to the same vineyards to help with the harvest?'

'Well, the local people turn up to help — it is fun,' she added, actually smiling. 'They understand the importance of the success of the harvest. We are lucky, we have loyal people, but perhaps that is because Monsieur Beaulieu pays them well and provides wonderful food for them.'

Laura wondered if Lucy Day would turn up again. In fact, the chances were that she would. If she really was living locally, why wouldn't she turn up to help with the harvest? She had done it before. Philippe's painting proved that. However, if she didn't turn up, that could indicate something more puzzling.

Reading the signposts as they motored on, Épernay was just 10 kilometres away, but the chauffeur veered off down a small country lane with the signposts telling of smaller villages. Every so often Laura glimpsed one of the beautiful Champagne houses, each quite outstanding in its own way. She wondered what Philippe's home would be like.

A few kilometres further on, she found out as the chauffeur slowed the car down to drive between palatial wrought-iron gates with the name *Champagne de Beaulieu* worked into an archway in ornate gold and black lettering.

Laura sat up straight, looking eagerly at the house at the end of the drive. It was a grand old building, three storeys high, which gave the impression of being even taller because of the stone steps and pillars leading up to a huge arched doorway. A magnificent wisteria covered the stonework, its vivid blue flowers contrasting against the grey, while the gardens were wild with trees burdened with fruit. Laura saw apple, plum and walnut trees before the car came to a halt at the foot of the steps.

'What an incredible house!' she breathed.

'*Oui*, it is almost one hundred and fifty years old.'

'I love it,' Laura murmured, more to herself than to anyone else as she slid from the car and gazed around, breathing in the fresh air that was rich in its own distinct fragrances. There was a sense of timelessness here, as if this was a place that the craziness of the world could not touch. Here was isolation and solitude and tranquillity. The quiet peaceful atmosphere stole into her heart.

'How many people live here?' Laura asked, looking up at the rows of windows, some with black, wrought-iron railed balconies.

'It is just Philippe and his mother,' the chauffeur replied, placing Laura's suitcase by her side. 'There are staff, of course, and employees, but they do not live in. They have their own homes close by.'

'So, who's here today?' Laura asked, feeling a jingle of nervousness in the pit of her stomach. 'Just Philippe and his mother?'

'No, not his mother. She has stayed on in Paris to preside over the exhibition. I will be picking her up in two or three days' time, when she calls me or when the start of harvesting is imminent.' She opened the car door. 'I will leave you in Monsieur Beaulieu's care. *Au revoir*, Laura.'

'No, wait!' Laura cried, not wanting to be left here alone with just Philippe. The prospect was suddenly very frightening. 'What about my hire car? You said . . . '

'*Oui*, I will arrange that for you.' She smiled. But there was something cool behind the smile, and Laura felt herself beginning to tremble. This was not a good situation and every bone in her body screamed at her to get back into that car and insist she be driven into the main town before it was too late.

But then the huge arched front door opened and Philippe stepped out from the house. He wore a white open-necked shirt tucked loosely into perfectly fitted jeans, his black hair was swept back, sleek and shining with health, his lightly tanned face was severe, his brows slightly lowered as if there were dark concerns going on in that brain of his.

Philippe stood there, very much lord and master of his grand domain. He looked loftily down at Laura; so tall, so powerful, his expression unfathomable. If he was happy to see her after all his trouble, it certainly didn't show on his face.

She was trembling slightly, feeling suddenly very small and vulnerable. But her nervousness was mingled with something else — an undeniable attraction towards this man, even though she barely knew him, even though he was possibly untrustworthy, even though her safety could be in jeopardy.

Despite all that, there was something about this man that drew her towards him.

Vaguely, she wondered if this was how Lucy Day had felt.

Among the Vines

Philippe came down the steps as the limousine pulled away, that boyish smile transforming his face, banishing that austere expression she had glimpsed at first. He held out his arms towards her.

'Laura! You came! I am a happy man!'

Her immediate instinct to run into those strong arms was swiftly dashed aside as her anger burned.

'I wish I could say the same. I didn't actually have much say in the matter. I was totally pressurised to get in the car and come here.'

Her anger clearly took him aback and she saw him halt in his tracks and rein back.

'I apologise.' His stance changed, his head actually hung low and he turned sad puppy-dog eyes at her.

Her heart did yet another flip. He obviously knew how appealing he looked, standing there, chastised, and Laura hated herself for succumbing to his charm.

'My excitement at capturing your loveliness in a painting has so over-whelmed me I forgot to consider your feelings. You are on holiday and you had plans. I have wrecked your itinerary.'

She folded her arms.

'Yes, you have,' she lied. 'I fully intended visiting some museums in Paris today.'

He glanced down at her suitcase.

'And that is your packed lunch?'

Colour flushed up her neck and into her cheeks.

'OK, so maybe that's not exactly true, but I was going to hire a car and explore.'

'And where better to start than this fantastic Champagne region,' he said, smiling again and spreading his arms wide to embrace this world that was his.

'Yes, it's beautiful, but — ' Before she

had chance to argue, he had picked up her suitcase and indicated for her to go ahead, up the steps and into his house. There was no point in arguing. Besides, she wanted answers to the mystery of Lucy Day, and she wasn't going to get them by being argumentative. With a resigned sigh, she walked up the steps towards those vast oak doors, her mind in turmoil.

The interior of the house oozed elegance in a style that harked back to the 1920s. The wide curved staircase looked to be straight out of an old Hollywood movie and on the first landing a beautiful stained-glass window sent shards of brilliant colour streaming across the hallway.

'This is stunning!' Laura exclaimed, overwhelmed by the grandeur and the steadfastness of the house. She turned and looked up at Philippe. 'Is this your family home? Did you grow up here?'

'Indeed,' Philippe said, moving to stand beside her, his arm just brushing lightly against hers. 'My great-grandfather built the house in the late 19th century and it has remained in my family ever since. Come.' He led the way into his living-room, which was a high-ceilinged room decorated in reds and creams with gilt mirrors, antique French cabinets and plush sofas. 'Make yourself comfortable, Laura. Can I get you some refreshment or something to eat?'

'Something long and cold would be good,' she said, risking a small smile at him, letting him know that he was forgiven for railroading her here.

'Please, relax. I shall not be long.'

Leaving her to her own devices for a few minutes, Laura explored the great Philippe Beaulieu's living-room, admiring his paintings and the classic French ornaments. Of all the furnishings, the framed pictures around his walls were the only modern items in the room. Laura thought they looked to be the work of Philippe himself — landscapes mainly, of the countryside and nature and winter scenes. All executed to perfection. There were photographs, too, some in black and white, all framed and standing on his sideboard and bureaus. She recognised his mother in some of the pictures, taken years ago. A tall, good-looking man was by her side. Judging from the likeness, Laura assumed it was Philippe's father. Older black and white photos were perhaps of his grandparents.

One photograph that particularly caught her eye was of a young couple and a little dark-haired boy in short trousers standing amongst vines lush with fruit, everyone smiling happily. Again, there was no mistaking Philippe's mother, so beautiful, and his father was handsome, too. She could understand where Philippe's good looks came from. She was still gazing at this photograph when Philippe returned.

'Is this you when you were little? You and your parents?'

'*Oui*, I was very cute, would you not say?' he remarked with a twinkle in his eye.

'Adorable!' she agreed lightheartedly.

He crossed the room and took the photograph from her, his smile becoming wistful.

'Sadly, my father is no longer with us. A motoring accident took him twelve years ago. It was a terrible shock to my mother.'

'And to you, too, no doubt,' she murmured softly, seeing the sadness in his eyes.

'Yes, to me also,' he said, acknowledging her light caress on his arm with an appreciative little smile.

As his attention was on the old photograph, Laura took the opportunity of studying his face close to. He was without doubt an extremely attractive man, his features were strong and well defined, his skin glowed with health beneath that light tan, and his eyes, framed by the longest black lashes, were the deepest blue. It was the sort of face that she could look at for ever and never grow tired of seeing.

With a sigh, Philippe replaced the

framed photograph on his polished sideboard.

'He was an exceptional man. We miss him. Not a day goes by that I do not wish that he was still here with us, running the business.'

'It can't be easy,' Laura remarked, guessing that to be an understatement, and her thoughts rested with Philippe, imagining the responsibility of running a multi-million pound business and having it thrust upon him when he was just in his early twenties.

Brightening, he said, 'It keeps me busy! And fortunately I have loyal employees, some who have been here since the days of my grandfather. For many they make champagne their whole lives. I am a lucky man.' He turned his attention to her as he added pointedly, 'A very lucky man!'

She wasn't quite sure what to say and she wondered whether that last comment had been directed at her personally. She hastily told herself that she was being fanciful and was relieved when he remembered he had her drink in his hand.

It was a long frosted glass, chinking with ice cubes and decorated with slices of lime. He apologised for holding on to it and watched her sipping it, his head tilted a little to the side, eyes shining.

'Is it to your liking, Laura?'

'Yes, thank you. It's lovely and refreshing,' she answered, trying not to let his continued attention disturb her. The fact that she was here alone with him was still causing alarm bells to clang in her head. Gorgeous and charming he might well be, but she didn't know him — and a girl had gone missing. She ought not to forget about that. Drawing his attention away from herself, she said, 'So champagne has been in your family for some generations?'

'Oh, yes, indeed. My great-grandfather and the local people dug out the deep cellars where our champagne is stored. An incredible accomplishment, as they are forty metres deep. Would you like to see, Laura? Could I give you a guided tour of my world?'

His enthusiasm caught her off guard and she answered without a moment's hesitation.

'Oh, I'd love that! Well, if you have time. I understand that the harvest could begin any day now.'

'Very soon,' he agreed. 'A day or two more of sunshine and then the grapes will be perfect. And perhaps this year it will be a vintage year.'

'What does that mean, exactly?' Laura asked, the mystery of Lucy Day slipping to the back of her mind again. 'I know it means an excellent year, but I don't know the technicalities of it.'

'Vintage, Laura, is a special year. When the crop is so good in quality and quantity that no other wines from other years are wanted in the blend,' he told her. 'Although, while it may be vintage for one house, it is not necessarily vintage for other houses — but usually, if it's a good year for one grower, it is good for all.'

97

'I see.' She nodded her head, enjoying the melodic sound of his voice; liking the flamboyant gestures that indicated his passion for his work. 'And then the bottles get stored, don't they?'

'*Oui.* We let it sleep for five years in our cellars. Three years is the very minimum, but I like Champagne de Beaulieu to rest for five years, and then . . . ' He kissed his fingers and blew the kiss into the air. '*Voilà!* Perfect!'

She smiled, understanding perfectly well his passion. She was equally as passionate about her own job: the importance of understanding a story with all its complications and being able to reconstruct it and tell it in a simplistic and accurate way that everyone would be able to understand. She opened her mouth to voice her thoughts, and then clamped her lips tightly shut. How could she suddenly admit to being a journalist — the scum of the earth, according to him?

'Come, let me show you,' he said,

taking the glass from her hand and setting it down on a low table. He strode to the door and she followed, aware of his commanding physique and the masculine grace of the man as he moved. She needed to remember why she was here, but it was so difficult — his presence had the power of totally distracting her from everything except him.

He led her through his house and out into the sunshine. At the rear of his house was a small cultivated garden with a crazy-paved patio and trellises of ivy and figs. A long bench table that would seat ten took up most of the area, but to the right of this, some way off, stood a compact industrial area with a variety of buildings. It marred only a small proportion of the panoramic view of the surrounding vineyards, and was clearly vital to the production of champagne.

Philippe led her in that direction, going first into what appeared to be the oldest building, a huge rustic barn.

Inside stood a circular wooden press.

'This, Laura, is our traditional press from my father's day, and his father before him,' Philippe informed her, one arm resting lightly on her shoulder. 'But we also have an automatic press that handles twice the capacity. It is important to press the grapes quickly so that we can get the juices into the vats and the temperature controlled. I will show you.'

He was off again, striding briskly out of the barn and into another much larger and more modern building. They were met immediately by a steep flight of iron stairs. Laura followed him, gripping the cool handrail, trying not to dwell on the cut of his well-fitting jeans as he ascended the stairs ahead of her. To her amazement they came out on to a gleaming stainless steel parapet that crossed a massive room with ten or twelve gigantic stainless steel vats below them.

Looking down Laura suddenly felt quite giddy, not least from the aromas filling the room. Her grip tightened on the handrail, and she deliberately avoided looking down.

A second later, Philippe's arm was around her shoulders. Not lightly as before, but holding her, steadying her.

'Are you all right, Laura? You are a little light-headed, *oui*?'

She nodded, still holding the rail tightly, but quite liking the sensation of his arm around her.

'I don't usually have a problem with heights. I think I'm OK now.'

'It is the smell of the carbon dioxide,' he explained, his eyes not leaving her face. 'It can have this effect. Plus, of course, we are ten metres up here, and this parapet gives the impression of walking on air. We shall go back outside — I was showing off. I am very proud of our state-of-the-art equipment. I apologise.'

'No, it's really interesting,' Laura protested, feeling her senses beginning to return to normal again. And it really was a new and fascinating environment for her. Under normal circumstances she would have had her notebook out and be taking notes on how the whole thing worked. But, of course, she wasn't going to be writing about this. She had to remember she sold shoes for a living, not stories. 'I'd love to know how it all works — I really would.'

'Are you just saying that?' he asked, one eyebrow arching suspiciously.

She promised him that she wasn't, and allowed him to 'show off' all he liked as he explained the technicalities of these temperature controlled, all singing, all dancing champagne-making gigantic utensils.

He talked about blending and riddling and degorging, and Laura listened, fascinated, eager to explore the deep dark cellars that he told her about, where those parts of the champagne-making process took place.

'All in good time,' Philippe said, eventually leading her back out into the warm sunlight. 'We will take a walk through the vines first. I will show you my beautiful Pinot Noir, Chardonnay and Pinot Meunier. 'He threw his hands up in the air suddenly, 'Ah! Laura! If only you loved champagne and not your soda water. It is the perfect drink for lovers.'

His eyes held hers a fraction too long and she turned aside, letting her hair form a curtain so that he couldn't see the colour rising in her cheeks. Of course he wasn't hinting at anything developing between them. Heaven forbid! She was here investigating the man and the missing Lucy Day. She certainly wasn't here to fall in love with him. Besides, she was nothing like the glamorous women he usually went out with, if the magazines were anything to go by.

Leaving the buildings behind, they strolled across a stretch of lush green grass, and the magnificent panorama opened up before them. For as far as she could see were field upon field of vines — a striped patchwork of fields, row upon row of grapevines, stretching for ever. The sight took her breath away.

'Oh! Philippe, this is incredible!'

'Champagne is the lifeblood of the area, and yes, it is quite breathtaking, is it not? It gives me great joy in just looking, knowing our prayers for a good harvest have been answered. I tell you, Laura,' he added with a lopsided little smile, 'a lot of prayers are said at this time of year. The growers send their mothers to church!'

'I can imagine!' she agreed, guessing he wasn't joking, as she had spotted many religious statues and grottos in the fields as she had travelled here. 'And it's all so neat — all these perfectly parallel rows!'

'We have to abide by the laws set down by the CIVC,' Philippe informed her, examining some of the green grapes at the start of the rows. 'Grapes for champagne must be grown and pruned and picked just so. You know they cannot be picked by machinery, for that would damage the skins. All champagne grapes are picked by hand.'

'That must be back-breaking work!' Laura remarked.

'Back killing!' He groaned. 'But there is no other way.'

He chatted on, telling her about the ages of the vines and the incredible depths of the roots, and how the wine is blended and the places it was exported to. It was fascinating and Laura hung on to every word, captivated by his enthusiasm and love for his work.

When he had finished talking, she simply remained there, drinking in the view, feeling almost intoxicated with the sheer beauty and silence and fragrances, oblivious to time passing. There was a warm breeze here in the open and her hair blew softly across her face. She pushed a lock back from her eyes, totally lost in this awe-inspiring world that Philippe had shown her.

She had no idea how long she stood there. It could have been minutes or it could have been hours. She felt as if she belonged here, as if this world had been waiting for her. But, of course, she didn't. She belonged back in England in her flat where the view looked down at a bus stop and a row of shops that didn't even sell champagne, and she shook herself from her daydream. She turned to find Philippe watching her, the strangest look in his eyes.

She smiled shyly.

'Sorry, I was miles away — or rather I wasn't. I was here, right here and just loving being here. It really is beautiful, Philippe. Thank you for showing me all this.'

His smile didn't come easily. It seemed that his expression had almost been set in stone as he stood watching her for some interminable time. But eventually his eyes crinkled just slightly in that way of his, and his lips formed that familiar smile. Quietly, he murmured, 'It is my pleasure.'

They strolled back to his house, not saying a word, but once inside Philippe rubbed his hands together gleefully and declared that he would make them some lunch.

'Can I help?'

'*Oui*. You can set the patio table with knives, forks and spoons. We shall eat outside, yes?'

'Sounds good to me,' Laura said agreeably, glancing around the room, not sure which drawer or cupboard would reveal the items she needed. His kitchen was a big old country farm-type kitchen with heavy oak dressers and a huge rustic table at the centre. Although charming and old fashioned in style, Laura noticed that Philippe's love for high-tech equipment didn't stop at champagne making. His kitchen was equipped with the necessary labour-saving devices to make cooking a pleasure.

With so many cupboards, however, she struggled to find the ones she needed for her part of the job. Philippe didn't offer any tips on where to look, and Laura thoroughly enjoyed delving through the cupboards, searching for cutlery, condiments and napkins.

As she busied herself, she cast a

cursory glance now and then at Philippe, finding that he was absorbed with cooking something that was beginning to smell wonderful.

He was clearly a natural in the kitchen and she couldn't help wonder if there was anything he wasn't good at!

Armed with rose-patterned plates and sturdy cutlery, Laura made her way out into the garden. She had only glimpsed it earlier, but now she saw that it was a delightful little oasis of plants and herbs in pots, climbing wild roses that hummed with bees and danced with brightly coloured butter-flies. The long wooden table stood beneath a wooden trellised veranda that was draped in grape vines and figs.

She had the feeling that these grapes were different from the vines — and edible. She picked one, delighting to find it sweet and delicious, unlike the grapes grown for champagne — their unpalatable taste had surprised her. After enjoying a few more grapes she got to work, setting the table so that she and Philippe were facing each other. A few minutes later he appeared with two glasses and a bottle of rosé wine.

'You might like this wine, Laura,' he said, pouring her a glass. 'It has a sweet taste and is wonderfully fruity. Please, sit down now and relax. Enjoy the day. I will bring lunch when it is ready.'

'If you insist!' She laughed, seating herself at the table and taking a sip of the wine. It was as good as he had said, and her glass was almost empty when he eventually returned carrying a tray of food. Laura breathed in the delicious aromas and felt her stomach rumble. 'Wow! This smells fantastic. I see you're a good cook as well as a good painter.'

'One tries.' He shrugged modestly, setting the food down.

He had cooked chicken in a mushroom sauce with a fresh tomato salad and crusty bread and butter. The simplicity of it made it quite perfect and she shook her head in appreciation.

'It looks wonderful. You really shouldn't have gone to all this trouble.'

His clear blue eyes met hers across the table.

'Cooking and eating are great pleasures to me, especially so when I am cooking for such a lovely young woman.'

Under the intensity of his gaze, Laura found herself lost for words. She managed a small smile and took a forkful of food. It tasted even better than it looked and she rolled her eyes in ecstasy.

'Fantastic!'

He smiled, poured himself a glass of wine and refilled her glass. He raised his in a toast.

'To a fruitful harvest!'

'To a fruitful harvest!' Laura agreed, chinking her glass against his, pleased that at least this was one toast she could drink to which didn't make her feel like a hypocrite!

Wine Tasting

Lunch was as delicious as it looked and smelled, and Laura finished every morsel on her plate, finishing off with strawberries and ice-cream. Philippe ensured that her glass was never empty and she was feeling a little light-headed by the time the meal was over.

Pushing his dessert dish to one side, he linked his fingers together beneath his chin and gazed across the table at her.

'Tell me about your life, Laura. Tell me about your family, your friends, the places you go.'

She thought for a moment, selecting her words carefully, wishing she could tell him about her job which was her passion and the first thing she normally chattered about whenever anyone asked about herself. It pained her to remain silent about it.

Deliberately she concentrated on her family. She had an older brother who was in the Navy and she had parents who both had good careers. Her father was an engineer who had also been in the Navy for a time, and her mother was a legal secretary. She told Philippe about them, making him smile as she recounted amusing incidents over the years. And she told him about her friends, the majority of whom worked at her newspaper, but because she was afraid he might link her with them, or take an instant dislike to them because they were journalists, she transferred them in her mind to her shoe shop. But, of course, she couldn't tell him of all the adventures she had experienced in the course of her work. The people they had met, the insane, funny and tragic events they had faced. And so she felt her conversation on that level fell flat, and bored him.

His eyes, however, never left her face, but she was positive there was a glazed look to them. He hardly seemed to be hanging on to her every word. It was more like his thoughts were elsewhere.

Her heart plummeted when he suddenly excused himself and headed back into the house. But moments later he returned with a sketchpad and a chunky well-worn pencil case. He sat opposite her again, eagerly flicking open the sketchpad and selecting the right pencil. Seconds later he was working his pencil over the white paper. As he drew, his eyes constantly flicked from the pad to her face and back again.

Laura gasped and covered her face with her hands.

'You're not drawing me now, are you? I must look a mess.'

'You look like you,' he answered, not halting for a second in his work, his hand flying across the page as if desperate to capture the moment. Then his gaze fixed directly on hers for a second as he said, 'And that is a good thing, trust me.'

The angle of his sketchpad was tilted upwards so that she couldn't see what he was drawing, but after a few minutes, and feeling more self-conscious by the second, she began to crane her neck to peep at what he was doing.

'Ah, ah! No, you cannot see,' he said, tilting the pad further away, a wickedly mischievous glint in his eye.

'Will I see it later?' Laura asked, settling back down.

He shrugged his broad shoulders.

'Perhaps.'

'Oh, that's mean.' Laura frowned, deliberately pouting.

He smiled.

'We shall see. Perhaps I will allow you a glimpse, but not if you keep that sulky expression on your face.

Deliberately she pulled a worse face at him.

'Ah, that is much better,' he joked, turning to a fresh sheet of paper and pretending to draw her contorted expression. She couldn't help but laugh and he captured that look instead.

He sketched for an hour or so, changing his position to view her from a different angle, or in different light. He repositioned her, sometimes sitting, sometimes standing. Sometimes looking directly at him, other times gazing away into the distance. Eventually he closed the sketchpad and crammed all his pencils back into their case. Laura stretched after being in the same position for some time, then raised her eyebrows hopefully at him.

'Are you going to show me now?'

'No,' he replied simply. 'These are just doodlings. There is nothing to see yet.'

Laura doubted that as she'd caught glimpses of the drawings and instantly recognised herself from his sketches. But there was no swaying him.

To her surprise he took her hand.

'Now I am going to show you our cellars. I am going to take you into another world. Please come.'

She couldn't resist even if she'd wanted to, and walking hand in hand with him back towards the industrialised area, she realised vaguely that she was making no progress at all in finding out about Lucy Day. However, the thought fluttered through her head and was gone in a flash. Right now, all that mattered was being close to Philippe and relishing in the sensation of her hand enclosed within his.

To her surprise, he led her towards a building that had a chic modern look to its architecture. Looking at it, Laura guessed it could only have been built in the last twenty years or so. It was stunningly elegant, with its double plate-glass doors etched with the Champagne de Beaulieu crest.

He released her hand to push open the glass door for her. She stepped into the cool interior and gazed in awe at a gleaming showroom that oozed elegance and style. Huge oak barrels cut in half were attached to the walls as show-pieces. A whole host of champagne-related ephemera was on display. Bottles of champagne in all their sizes stood on high, ranging from normal-sized bottles to ones of gigantic proportions.

Philippe reeled off a list of names from a magnum, that held the equivalent to two wine bottles, to rehoboam which held six, to nebuchadnezzar, holding twenty.

'The bottles can get even bigger,' Philippe explained, smiling at her astonished face, 'but they would be impossible to lift and pour.'

'And drink!' she exclaimed.

'It has been tried!' he assured her, strolling towards the rear of the grand showroom. 'This, as you can see, Laura, is our public face, where our visitors and tourists will come. Melissa, our chauffeur, works here as our receptionist and guide when we have our open days or special guests.'

'A handy girl to have around?' Laura remarked, hoping her words didn't sound as acid to him as they did to her.

'Absolutely!' he agreed, his expression giving away nothing.

Laura nodded, trying not to feel a twang of envy at Melissa's importance to the Beaulieu family and business.

The woman was very clearly part of the scene and irreplaceable. The memory of her passed through her mind, reminding her not to start getting fanciful ideas about him. They were from different worlds — and she was here to try to solve a mystery, not to kindle a romance.

She strolled along beside him, totally nonplussed that he seemed to prefer walking freely, his hands at his sides or gesticulating at this or that object placed on show.

He took delight in telling her all about the artefacts and reeling off a host of interesting anecdotes, then finally he clasped his hands together and said, 'But now, we will go down into the cellars. I hope you will not be too cold. The temperature is much cooler down there.'

'I'll let you know,' Laura answered, wondering if he had taken Lucy Day down into his cellars. That was who she had to concentrate on. There was absolutely no future in their liaison and she'd better not forget it. He was from another world — one filled with beautiful women. Besides, in an hour or two she would be out of here — probably none the wiser about Lucy Day at the rate she was going — but possibly with her heart in tatters if she didn't keep her guard up.

There was a small door at the back of the showroom. Philippe held it open for her, a slightly puzzled expression on his face.

'Laura? Is everything all right? You look perturbed.'

'No, I'm fine,' she said, mustering up a smile. 'Can't wait to see these cellars.'

'You must be very careful,' he said, stepping in front of her now that she was close. 'The steps down are quite steep, and we have only candlelight to light our way until we reach the cellars. Then we have sodium lights which do not affect the temperature as electric lights would.'

Once through the door, the atmosphere changed dramatically. From the brightness of the showroom they were plunged into shadow. The corridor was simply brick walls, lit by fat candles flickering from niches in the brickwork. Then rounding a corner they were faced with a steep stone staircase, a hundred or more steps cut from the chalky white stone, leading down into the arched brick caverns.

'Oh, my goodness!' Laura breathed as she looked down and glimpsed what lay waiting — thousands upon thousands of bottles of champagne.

Philippe touched her elbow.

'Take care on the steps, Laura. I shall go first. Please take your time.'

They descended slowly, the candles flickering as they disturbed the air — air that was distinctly cooler down here, and silent. Laura felt that when she spoke it should be in a whisper. This was a quiet world, where the champagne slept until it was ready. A dream-like world, unreal, magical.

Reaching the bottom of the steps, Philippe turned and smiled at her. The smile made her heart leap unexpectedly. Then he walked on a little and Laura followed, totally in awe at the surroundings. Here was a catacomb of silent passageways, lit now by sodium lights that bathed everything in a soft hue of orange.

'We have three kilometres of tunnels, Laura,' Philippe said, speaking softly. 'During the second world war they were used for the villagers to take refuge in.'

'It's amazing,' she breathed, hearing only her own quiet voice and their echoing footsteps as they walked past the deep arched brick tunnels that reached far back and were filled with bottle upon bottle of champagne, lying there like the ripples of the ocean, gathering dust, silent and still.

'You are not too cold?' he asked, and when she shook her head he added, 'The temperature is the same down here the whole year round. We have a hundred thousand bottles of champagne down here, Laura. You see how they are marked and labelled.'

'Yes, I see,' she murmured, curious as to why some bottles were stored in racks. She asked him about this.

'Each Champagne house has its own unique style in how they keep the wine, how it is turned,' he explained, examining a bottle. 'For a number of weeks the bottles are held on racks, neck down, and turned just a little three or four times a day. Some Champagne houses turn every single bottle precisely a quarter — by hand. Other Champagne houses will have their wine on pallets and these are turned by computerisation. It is called riddling.'

'Every bottle?' She gasped, deciding that job must be like painting the Forth Bridge.

'*Oui*, every bottle! We prefer the old traditional ways in some things.' He looked steadily at her and his eyes shone with pride. 'In this part of the process I follow my father's ways and his father before him.'

'This is unbelievable,' she murmured,

realising suddenly that the world really didn't know Philippe at all. This was what he was passionate about, not being seen out on the town with beautiful women. At that moment, she saw it in his face. She touched his arm gently and looked up into those clear blue eyes. 'It's wonderful, Philippe. I love it.'

He said nothing, but his face shone with happiness. He strolled on with Laura at his side, marvelling at the sight of all these bottles, trying to comprehend the years of work, the sweat and toil and worry that had gone into producing all this champagne.

'It's just fantastic when you think about it,' she murmured, her voice hushed in reverence to these sleeping bottles. 'Every single bottle here will one day be a part of someone's special celebration — a wedding maybe, or an anniversary, or the birth of a baby.'

He simply nodded knowingly. As they wandered through the passageways, they came across the cellar-master,

Raymond, a man in his sixties at least, whom she was introduced to. Philippe spoke in French to the man and Raymond beamed a wide smile at her and shook her hand until it ached.

'It is Raymond's job to blend the champagne, and that is the art which differentiates between all the many different champagnes which come out of France. He worked for my father and, as a boy, with my grandfather.'

'How is it blended?' Laura asked curiously.

'Blending is based on taste, first impressions,' Philippe said, drawing up his shoulders and letting them fall. 'It is like a painting, like a Picasso, there is no rigid structure.'

Raymond spoke then, in his native tongue, which Philippe translated for her.

'Raymond says when we blend the whole team get together. It is like the election of the Pope. We are locked in a room and we don't get out until we are finished. The only thing missing is the little wisp of smoke.'

Laura laughed, and bidding 'Au revoir' to the cheerful cellar master, Philippe took her elbow and led her back up another flight of stairs, along another long corridor and finally into another large room. This room, however, was vastly different to the tranquillity of the cellars. This room was filled with noise, with the clink and rattle of bottles and the hum of a conveyor belt as these champagne bottles went through more processes.

The chatter of the half-dozen workers was barely audible above the mechanical sounds and Laura had to strain her ears to catch what Philippe was telling her.

'This is where we de-gorge the bottles, cork and label them, and pack them into cases,' Philippe explained, going into detail as Laura quizzed him on the process. In between his explanations, he stopped to chat to each of his employees, and each time introduced Laura to them.

Finally he led her from the noisy work-room, along yet another corridor — more subtly lit this time — and into a silent, elegant room with alcoves in its white walls containing racks of champagne and a long glass table with leather and chrome stools. Champagne flutes were lined up down its centre.

'And this room, Laura, is where we ply our honoured guests with vintage champagne and hope they will appreciate it, having now a better understanding of how it is made, and the love that goes into it.'

Laura perched herself on one of the stools and smiled at him. Unreservedly she said, 'I would love a glass of champagne, Philippe. Thank you.'

She felt slightly tipsy when they eventually stepped out into the bright sunshine again. They had spent an hour tasting different champagnes, with Philippe being incredibly hospitable in opening bottle after bottle, just so that she could compare the tastes. Educating her to the elegance of his world.

She had enjoyed the intimacy of simply being there with him, sampling this bubbly liquid as if there was no tomorrow, enjoying the close proximity of this attractive man. There was a delicious rosy glow to everything now, and Laura knew that it wasn't all down to the champagne intoxicating her.

They strolled back towards his house, with Laura now armed with her new vocabulary of champagne-related words and terms, and she still had a barrage of questions to put to Philippe so that her understanding of the champagne business was clear in her head.

She stopped herself abruptly, afraid she was slipping into journalist mode, needing to know the ins and outs of everything so that she could write effectively about it. She hoped she hadn't already given herself away. She hoped he hadn't recognised the similarities of her questions to how other journalists might speak to him.

'Oh! I'm sorry,' she said, trying to sound giddy. 'I just find it all so interesting. I'm babbling on. Ignore me.'

His black eyebrows joined in a frown.

'Not at all, it is good to be inquisitive. You have a questioning mind, Laura. I hope you don't mind me saying so, but I think you could find a more challenging career than the one you have.'

'Such as?' she asked invitingly, tilting her head to look at him.

He thought for a moment then said, 'A barrister, perhaps?'

She laughed, quite flattered by his suggestion.

'I wish!'

'Do not underestimate yourself, Laura. I think you could do anything you set your heart on.'

Perhaps now was the right time to come clean and tell him the truth. That she wasn't a shoe-shop assistant at all, but a journalist. Surely he wouldn't object to her now that he had got to know her and, so it seemed, to quite like her. She was just about to broach the subject when she spotted a car turning into his drive. She saw at once that Melissa was at the wheel.

'Here comes your girl Friday.'

'Indeed,' he said, looking slightly puzzled. He quickened his step, leaving Laura a little behind in his wake as he hurried along to meet her.

Laura didn't know whether to hang back and let them talk in private, but then Philippe waved at her to join them. The champagne made her slightly wobbly and she hoped neither of them noticed, but quite obviously they did, making Laura feel totally at a disadvantage now. Melissa being so crisp and smart — and sober!

Philippe seemed to be trying not to laugh as she caught up with him. He had a set of keys in his hand, which Melissa had just given to him. He instantly pocketed them.

'Ah, Laura, Melissa has arranged this hire car for you as you requested, but I do not think you are in a fit condition to drive it just at the moment.'

'Probably not,' she had to agree, then giving the other woman a polite smile, and trying to act soberly and in control, added, 'Thank you for arranging the car. Is the hire agreement in there? I'll need to know where to return it and pay for it.'

Philippe dismissed her worries with the wave of his hand.

'All that is taken care of. Do not concern yourself with this, Laura.' He spoke to Melissa then. 'I hadn't realised you were bringing the car just now, because I, too, am not sober enough to drive you home. I apologise.'

The woman raised her slender shoulders and let them fall.

'I shall walk. The day is beautiful. I shall enjoy it.'

True to her word she set off, but not before she had placed a kiss on Philippe's cheek. As she turned to go, Philippe suddenly realised he had something else to say to her and this time it obviously wasn't meant for Laura's ears.

'Melissa!' he called to halt her. And then he spoke to Laura.

'Please, go inside, Laura, and make yourself at home, I shall only be a minute or two.'

Feeling like she was being dismissed, she hesitated, but the pair of them stood patiently, waiting for her to disappear before they got into any conversation. Pretending she didn't feel miffed, Laura turned and headed for the door, acutely aware that not a single word passed between Philippe and Melissa until she had closed the large oak door behind her.

Knowing she shouldn't, but unable to help herself, she hurried through to his living-room which overlooked the front gardens and drive. Standing back from the window, hidden behind the curtain, she peeped out at them and craned her ears to try and catch what they were saying. The window was open a little to allow the fresh air in, and she could just catch the odd word or two. And two of the words she overheard were Lucy Day.

They parted and Laura raced through to his kitchen, heart thumping, where she busied herself by making a coffee, although she only got as far as filling the kettle, having no idea where he kept his coffee jar.

Her thoughts were spinning, but she focused on the mundane, asking him where his coffee and cups were kept, avoiding his eyes until she was positive her guilt over eavesdropping was masked. Although she wasn't the one who should be feeling guilty. She wasn't involved in the disappearance of a young English girl. That was him.

Why, though, had he mentioned it to Melissa now? Were his suspicions aroused as to what she was really doing here? Had he guessed that she wasn't who she said she was? Maybe he knew all along that she was the Laura who had been writing about the missing girl in her local newspaper month after month.

She felt confused and anxious. She

really didn't know this man. Yes, he was charming and good looking, but so were a lot of villains.

He reached above her head and she felt suddenly enveloped by him. It was nevertheless a pleasant sensation, despite being on her guard again now. He took a jar of coffee from the cupboard and placed it in her hands. Then he found two mugs and stood them next to the kettle.

'I take mine strong and black, *merci*.'

'Coming up!' she said, sounding cheery, but inside her heart was racing. 'That was nice of Melissa to arrange a hire car for me. Does she have a long way to walk home?'

'A kilometre at the most,' he said, leaning against a cupboard, arms folded, watching her. 'She lives quite close by, in a little village near here.'

Laura felt suddenly that she hadn't much to lose. As the kettle came to the boil and she made the coffee, she took a deep breath and broached the subject head on.

'Yes, I wanted to explore the villages around this area. There's a village called Pierry, isn't there? I remember at your exhibition your mother was telling a woman who'd bought one of your paintings that the girl in the picture lived in Pierry.'

His eyes narrowed for the briefest of moments, and then he shrugged.

'That is probably so. My mother tends to know these things.'

'Now, which painting was it?' Laura deliberately pondered. 'Oh, yes, it was the one with the dreamy-looking girl in — the one I particularly liked.'

'Ah, yes,' he agreed, fetching milk from the refrigerator. 'Do you take your coffee white?'

'Please,' she said, studying him. He looked as if he was making time to think, to think fast. 'You said it was a French student, didn't you?'

'Did I? Possibly, if you say so, though I confess I cannot remember. Is this enough milk?'

'Perfect, thank you. But your mother

said the girl in the picture was an English girl who had run away from home and was living with her lover in this neck of the woods.'

He took his coffee and carried it to the solid-looking table at the centre of the room. He sat down, sipping at the rich liquid as if he hadn't a care in the world.

'If that is what my mother said, then that must be correct. My mother involves herself with the local people much more than I.'

Laura pressed on.

'I wonder if I know the girl. Do you know her name?'

He uttered a little laugh.

'Laura, I know England is not a very big country, but the odds that you may know her are very slim. And if I ever knew her name, I have forgotten it now. Come, sit down, drink your coffee and tell me if you are still feeling a little heady after your taste of champagne.'

She carried her mug over to the big oak table and sat opposite him. He was so matter-of-fact about this whole Lucy Day thing, that if she hadn't just overheard him saying her name, she would have thought he really did know nothing about her. But he had said her name — he had distinctly said Lucy Day to Melissa. Unless he'd said lovely day — perhaps she was hearing things. Perhaps all this was starting to get to her. Or perhaps it was because she was tipsy.

She ran her hand over her eyes.

'Actually, Philippe, I'm not feeling too bright. I could actually do with sitting quietly for a while.'

'Come with me,' he said at once, rising from his seat. 'Bring your coffee.'

She did as she was told and found herself following him through to the hall and up the wide staircase. She stopped dead in her tracks.

'Er . . .'

He glanced back over his shoulder.

'We have many guest rooms, Laura, I would like to offer you one so that you can relax, close your eyes and come back downstairs when you are ready.' He smiled. 'That is all I am offering, Laura. My intentions are honourable, I promise you.'

He must have said lovely day, she decided, feeling her suspicions evaporate. His hand was extended towards her, and willingly she caught up with him on the stairs, slipped her hand into his, and allowed him to lead her upstairs towards her room.

A Revelation

Phillipe indulged her with a short conducted tour of the upstairs rooms, pointing out which were his and his mother's bedrooms, and then an en-suite guest room, which he invited her to use.

The bathroom was a delight, with its massive cast-iron bath on ornate little legs which looked deceptively antique. The luxurious fitments told Laura it was state-of-the-art luxury. The bedroom, fresh and airy, was typically French with the solid furnishings and a double bed with a mattress and pillows that were feather-light and springy.

'Please, be at home, Laura,' he said, crossing the room to the door. He hesitated for a second and Laura thought she sensed a slight wistfulness to his smile as he closed the door and returned downstairs.

She sank down on to the bed, her thoughts wandering, indulging in a little fantasising of what it might be like to be in Philippe's arms. Despite all her reserves about the man, there was no denying how handsome he was. It was more than just looks that attracted her, however. There was something about him that drew her to him. It was a new and exciting sensation that she wasn't familiar with.

Kicking off her shoes, she stretched out on the luxurious bed and allowed her eyes to close for a moment or two, wondering dreamily whether this could be love.

She awoke to the sounds of birds calling to each other. It was the sound of evening and the starlings were returning home to roost. It was a familiar sound that she recognised from summer nights in England. Through the window she saw that the sun had moved around and a deep golden glow was shining through the window while the air on her skin was cool.

She sat up quickly. Peering at her watch, she was horrified to find it was almost eight o'clock at night. She had slept the afternoon away. Still groggy with sleep, she slipped her shoes back on and headed for the stairs. The smell of something delicious cooking was wafted through the house.

She headed for the kitchen first, but there was no sign of Philippe, although the cooker was on and there was plenty of evidence that someone had been preparing food. She looked into the living-room next, again without finding him, and so she explored the rest of the downstairs rooms, discovering the most elegant of dining-rooms with a dark mahogany oval table in its centre, set perfectly for two with crystal glasses and candles just waiting to be lit.

It was clear that he was expecting a guest for dinner, and she had definitely overstayed her welcome. She couldn't help but wonder whether his guest was Melissa. Ridiculously, Laura felt a pang of jealousy, but clearly they were right for each other. Both beautiful people, working closely together. What could be more perfect?

She pulled herself together and rallied her thoughts. She was being irrational. It had absolutely nothing to do with her what Philippe and Melissa got up to. What she had to do now was find him, take charge of the hire car, drive into Épernay and book into a hotel. However, locating him in a place this size was the problem.

She eventually found another door, and cautiously eased it open. Peeping in, she saw that it was a glass-walled conservatory. But it was more than that. It was the studio where the celebrated artist Philippe Beaulieu created his masterpieces. There were canvasses and paintings all around the walls, stacked side by side, overlapping. Canvasses of all sizes, some completed, some half finished, some covered in sheets. And in the centre was the great man himself.

Philippe stood working at an easel, his back to the door, oblivious and too lost in his work to be aware that Laura was watching him. The evening sunlight bathed him in a golden hue so that he was almost silhouetted against the light. The vision of him, Laura thought, was worthy of a painting in itself.

She stood silently, watching him at work. He and his painting were angled so that she couldn't quite see what he was working on, although from what she could glimpse, and the fact that his open sketchpad was propped up nearby, she had a feeling that it could be her. For the moment he was too caught up in his work to be aware that she was there and so Laura revelled in the moment.

Her breathing was shallow, soft, not wanting to break his concentration, not wanting to spoil the joy of standing here simply gazing at him.

The revelation stunned her. Was it possible that she had fallen in love with this man in so short a time?

As she stood there, gazing at him, she knew the answer.

Then, even though she had not made a sound, he turned and saw her, and smiled. Her heart did a ridiculous kind of somersault in her breast, and she knew that she was smiling back at him and her heart was pounding.

'At last, my sleeping beauty has awoken!'

Laura drew up her shoulders and let them fall.

'I'm so sorry. I only meant to close my eyes for a minute.'

He put his brush into water and moved away from his work, barring her view, although she snatched a little glimpse and became even more certain that it was of her.

'It is no problem,' Philippe said. 'I have filled the time usefully. I have been painting.'

'Can I see what you've been working on?' Laura asked hopefully, trying to peer around his broad physique.

He waggled his finger from side to side.

'Ah, no! It is not ready for eyes to

look on except mine. I trust you will not be tempted to peek.'

She was wildly curious.

'What are you painting?'

He wiped his hands on a cloth.

'Just ideas. I toy with ideas. I like to see what might work and what does not. There is nothing special there for you to see, not yet.'

She felt mischievous and excited.

'Is it me?'

'You do not need to know.' He laughed, ushering her towards the door.

She did her best to escape his clutches and see for herself, but he was determined she wouldn't see his work in progress.

'If it satisfies your curiosity, Laura, then I will tell you, it is you. But it is not ready for anyone but myself to look upon it.' A frown creased his forehead then. 'It is not my best work at the moment. I still have much to do. I have not captured what I am after — it remains elusive still.'

Laura felt slightly deflated, guessing

that it was because she was nowhere near as beautiful or interesting as the other people he had painted. He should have listened to her in the first place.

But on the other hand, it might not be that at all. Painting a picture was like writing a story — it was that creative process. It was the same for her. She hated anyone reading her articles over her shoulder at work when she was just drafting them out. She could quite understand why he wouldn't want anyone commenting on anything that was nowhere near finished. But of course she couldn't voice any of that, even though she was on the verge of saying that she understood completely. Instead, she clammed up so suddenly that he cast her a curious glance, one eyebrow arched expectantly. Laura turned away, positive he would think her a total dummy.

Once outside of his studio with the door firmly shut behind them, he strolled along the hallway and stopped by the stairs.

'I need to shower and change, Laura,' he said, indicating his paint-spattered hands and clothes.

Disappointment flooded through her as she realised it was time for her to leave. She swallowed hard, determined to leave with dignity. He would never know that he had got under her skin and that walking out of his life was going to be the hardest thing she had ever done.

She forced a smile.

'Yes, of course. Don't let me hold you up any further. If you'd let me have the hire car keys, I'll leave you in peace. I thought I'd drive into Épernay and stay there overnight. I'll head back to Paris in the morning, or maybe see some more of the countryside here first.'

A look of total remorse spread over his face as he swiftly exclaimed.

'But I have made dinner!'

Laura's mouth fell open. That beautifully set table was for her — not Melissa or some other woman!

'I . . . I couldn't possibly . . . '

'And I have still more paintings to do of you — and I would love you to be here for the harvest, at least for a day or two. Please change your mind, Laura.' The puppy-dog eyes were back. 'I promise I have not cooked frogs' legs or escargot for our meal.'

She couldn't stop the gurgle of laughter that bubbled up inside of her. Deep in her heart she felt as if she'd been given a reprieve, and she couldn't have felt happier. Deliberately she stopped herself from imagining how very much worse their parting was going to be after she'd spent even more time with him. But for now, staying here with Philippe was the thing she wanted most in the world.

'You're very kind, Philippe,' she said graciously, not allowing her true feelings to burst through. Calmly she continued. 'You've already cooked me lunch and bought me dinner last night, and you don't really know me.'

'I am trying to get to know you,

Laura,' he said, looking searchingly at her. 'But I feel that I have not even scratched the surface yet.'

She lowered her eyes, guilt marring the moment.

'That's true. But what happens if you get to know the real me and you don't like what you find?'

A frown darkened his gaze.

'You have a dark secret?'

'Maybe,' she murmured, looking back at him, reminding herself of why she was really here. 'Do you?'

His lips curved into a curious little smile.

'Should I have?'

'You tell me!'

His eyes narrowed.

'*Mais oui*, I have a thousand secrets. I am a private man, despite what the papers say. They plaster what they think is the real me across their pages. But they don't understand the man behind that image. I think sometimes it drives them mad. They would love to know what makes me tick, but they are shallow and only see what to them is obvious.'

Laura baulked at admitting that she was one of this hated breed, wondering whether he actually knew. But now wasn't the moment to come clean. Perhaps over dinner she would pluck up the courage to tell him the truth.

'You will stay for dinner, Laura?' he asked again, a pleading glimmer in his eyes. 'And if you can spare the time, I really would love you to be here for the start of the harvest. I think you would love the experience.'

The prospect of staying here for a few more days thrilled her. Not least because she loved being in his company, but also because she still hadn't got to the bottom of Lucy Day's disappearance. But she couldn't help but wonder about his reasons. Either he did know she was a journalist and wanted to keep a close eye on her, or he liked her.

She hoped it was the latter, although she couldn't understand why. He never seemed to be short of female company — unless, of course, that was just media gossip, which was the point he seemed to be constantly making.

'I really don't know what to say, Philippe.'

'Simple! Just say you will stay with me for a day or two.'

Her head felt like it was spinning. To stay for the harvest might possibly solve the mystery. If the girl was here last year grape picking, then she might come back again this year. But as Laura prepared to accept Philippe's invitation, she knew in her heart that that wasn't her main reason for agreeing to stay. The main reason was here standing before her, a hopeful look in his anxious blue eyes, a look that was melting her heart.

'It's very kind of you, Philippe.'

His face dropped.

'But . . . ?'

'No, I was going to stay. It's really kind of you, and yes, I'll stay a little longer. I just don't want to impose and outstay my welcome, so just show me the door when you're sick of the sight of me!'

He looked for a second as if he was going to take her in his arms, but then his gaze flicked down to his paint-spattered hands and seemed to change his mind.

'I can't imagine I shall become sick of the sight of you, Laura. It is refreshing to have you here. I am a happy man.'

Something plummeted inside of her as she realised that he wouldn't be saying that if he knew she was a journalist, investigating his involvement with a missing girl.

He started up the stairs.

'We shall eat in one hour. If you wish to take a shower or a bath, please do so. I will see you for dinner at nine-thirty.'

She nodded, blinking rapidly as her eyes started to sting. He was a lovely man and she was here under false pretences.

Laura took the opportunity of soaking in that deep luxurious bath and afterwards sorted through her suitcase for something to wear. The most sophisticated dress she'd packed was a sky blue chiffon calf-length dress which she'd packed purely because it didn't crease. She slipped into some low-heeled sandals and clipped her hair up to give a more elegant look.

As she got ready she battled with her conscience. She really needed to tell Philippe the truth about her work. Before things went any further, she needed to pick her moment and come clean. Surely he would realise that she wasn't some paparazzi reporter out to dish the dirt. She groaned. That might be exactly the way he saw things. He might think she'd tricked her way into his confidence and into his home under false pretences, which, in a way was true. She felt ashamed to admit it. He was going to be furious and would hate her. She couldn't hope for anything other than that reaction.

With a heavy heart she checked her appearance in the full-length mirror. She looked reasonably elegant and wouldn't be out of place in his glorious dining-room. Although her eyes lacked sparkle, knowing that this was all based on lies. With her thoughts in turmoil, she went down to dinner.

She found him in the kitchen, stirring something in a saucepan.

'Something smells good.'

He turned and his blue eyes swept over her.

'Ah! How beautiful you look!'

She felt her cheeks glow.

'Thank you. You look rather fetching yourself!'

He shrugged.

'A little something I threw on.'

She laughed at his casual air. He had dressed quite formally for dinner in black trousers and a soft white silk shirt, left open at the neck.

'Can I help with anything?'

'No, it is all in hand. Please, go

through and make yourself comfortable. I shall bring the soup through in a minute.'

Her stomach rumbled and she didn't argue. In the dining-room he had lit the candles and there was a warm cosy ambience now that the long velvet curtains were drawn against the approaching night.

She sat down, aware that butterflies were dancing in her tummy. She gazed at the loveliness of the room, at the care he had taken in placing the silver cutlery and sparkling glasses in just the right place. There was a bottle of red wine — the same that they'd had in the restaurant last night. It was already uncorked and breathing. Small soft bread rolls sat in a basket with curls of butter in a little dish. It was perfect.

Ridiculously, even though he was only in the next room, she awaited his appearance with eagerness. She wanted to see him again, wanted him here in this room, beside her. She longed to see his face again, see his smile, hear his voice. It was crazy and, she realised, dangerous. At this rate she was going to leave here with a broken heart.

When he entered minutes later with two bowls of steaming soup, she tried to mask her true feelings, tried not to let her gaze linger too long on his face, or to hang on to his every word. Instead she attempted to sound blasé and pretend that the only thing she was interested in was this soup.

'Mmm! This smells absolutely wonderful. What sort is it?'

'It is tomato and herb,' he told her, sitting opposite and pouring the wine. 'The ingredients are all home-grown.'

'You didn't rustle this up yourself while I was asleep, did you?'

'I would like to say that I did, but that would be a lie,' he admitted. 'My mother made it. She makes a whole pot and then freezes it. All I did was defrost and re-heat. Not so fantastic.'

'Well, it's delicious!' Laura confirmed.

He smiled as he raised his glass.

'*Bon appétit!*'

She chinked her glass against his, and at that moment their eyes met and for a second it seemed that time stood still. And then Laura looked swiftly away.

'*Bon appétit!*' she murmured, afraid that he would read her thoughts and know that she was falling head over heels in love with him.

A strange kind of silence descended on them, as if they had both seen something in each other's eyes, and both determined not to accept or acknowledge it. Philippe sounded quite blasé himself now.

'I'm glad you like the soup. My mother will be pleased to know that.'

'When is she coming back?' Laura asked, keeping the conversation light.

'Tomorrow evening. And the harvest begins the day after, I think.'

'That must be exciting,' Laura remarked, savouring the soup which was extremely delicious. 'After a year of growing and tending and nurturing, finally to begin the harvest.'

'Exciting, yes, and terrifying!' Philippe said. 'We spend a lot of time praying at this time of year, for sunshine, for rain, for the rain to stop.' He looked serious for a moment. 'I heard today there is a storm in the Atlantic threatening to blow this way. We are praying that it will miss the region.'

'Gosh! Yes, that wouldn't be good,' Laura acknowledged. 'I'm sure it will blow itself out before it reaches here. It's very rare to get hurricanes in this part of the world, isn't it?'

'Yes, that is true. I am sure I am worrying over nothing.'

The conversation flowed easily then, as Philippe talked freely about his hopes and fears for the harvest and what it meant to the local people and those who worked for him. Laura loved listening to him, just the sound of his voice made her glow inwardly with pleasure. But it was his passion for his work that was infectious, and before long she was as excited and terrified about the success of the harvest as he.

The main course was a beef casserole with meat that melted in the mouth. This, he explained, had been made fresh by his own fair hands although the dessert — raspberries soaked in a sweet liqueur and served on a light sponge cake with cream — was another of his mother's creations that he'd simply had to defrost. Nevertheless it was divine and Laura told him so.

Apart from that one awkward moment when their eyes had met, the conversation throughout the meal was light and easy, chatting like old friends, laughing and enjoying each others' company, feeling as if they had been friends for ever.

They took coffee in the lounge, sharing the sofa, albeit at different ends. Philippe stretched out his long legs, relaxing his head back against the cushions, his eyes closed for a moment. Laura kicked off her sandals and curled her legs under her, perfectly comfortable in his presence.

'Do you have a boyfriend back home, Laura?' Philippe asked, his eyes still closed.

She glanced at him, quite startled. His eyes flicked open and the question was still there in his gaze.

'Well, actually, no, not at the moment. I'm so busy with work . . . ' she stopped abruptly.

'Ah, yes, selling shoes.'

She took a sip of her coffee, wondering if he did actually know her true profession and was just leading her on. She knew that she really ought to tell him now that she was a journalist. She took a deep breath.

'Actually, Philippe, there are some professions where work has to come first. You obviously know that, even though the newspapers and magazines like to show you off as some kind of playboy. But not every newspaper treats people like that.'

'Don't they indeed!' He silenced her, speaking unusually sharply. 'I have no time for the media with their tittle-tattle

159

and their assumptions. They assume and then they destroy.'

Taken aback by the bitterness in his voice, Laura curiously asked, 'What have they destroyed?'

'Everything!' he uttered, getting to his feet, crossing the room to nowhere in particular, like some angry beast in a cage. 'They take the innocent and turn it into something tarnished, tainted. It is like they take some malicious pleasure in hurting people.'

'Have you been hurt?' she asked warily, saddened by the change in mood, but curious to know more.

'Long ago,' he said, turning aside and pouring himself a brandy. 'Now they just infuriate me. They are scandal mongers. They take peoples' lives apart and ruin them just to sell their papers. It sickens me, Laura. It sickens me to the very soul!'

All her good intentions to come clean suddenly evaporated, even though she was desperate to tell him — to prove to him — that not all journalists were like the ones he had encountered. In fact, she didn't know any who behaved like that, certainly not on her paper.

She opened her mouth to try and tell him this, but the words that she needed weren't there. Instead she desperately wanted to know what had happened to him to make him so bitter towards the press.

'What happened, Philippe?'

He stood with his back to her and she could see his breathing was deep, as if he was struggling to get his emotions under control. He remained looking away from her as he spoke. His voice was quiet, controlled — matter of fact.

'I was engaged to be married four years ago. Her name was Colette. She was a very sweet, naïve girl.' He turned and faced her. 'I loved her dearly.'

Laura felt a stab to her heart. Somehow she kept the feeling from showing in her face.

'And?' she asked flatly.

He took a deep breath.

'For some reason the papers seemed

to take pleasure in ensuring every photo they took of me, in whatever situation, included some other female. Colette believed everything she saw and read. It drove her crazy with jealousy.'

'She ended your engagement?' Laura presumed.

He took a gulp of brandy before answering.

'That is one way of saying it,' he said, his chest expanding as if he needed to take a deep, steadying breath before continuing. 'As I said, jealousy drove her crazy. One night, after accusing me of all sorts of infidelities, she stormed off and crashed her car. She was killed instantly.'

'Oh, my goodness!' Laura gasped, shocked by his revelation. No wonder he hated newspapers.

Without another thought, she crossed the room to him and wrapped her arms around him, holding him close. His arms encircled her in return and his head leaned heavily on her shoulder. She could feel his heart hammering against her throat, and sensed that his grief was still raw as he struggled not to break down and weep.

'I apologise,' he said softly after some moments, easing away from her, clearly embarrassed.

Laura stepped back, searching his face, seeing the pain — feeling his pain herself.

'There's nothing to apologise for. I'm so sorry for your loss,' she breathed.

He gave a small, little-boy-lost kind of smile and murmured with a shrug, 'Now you see why I have no time for these reporters. You understand my loathing for them?'

'Yes,' she uttered in a tiny voice. She did understand why he hated journalists — she understood perfectly. But the saddest thing was — she was one of them.

'You Are Perfect'

Laura awoke the next morning, wondering for a moment where she was. Then the events of last night came rushing back. Uppermost in her mind was the fact that Philippe's fiancée had died, and it had broken his heart.

Their evening had drawn to a close shortly after that revelation. Although Philippe had rallied himself and turned the conversation around, doing his best to brighten the mood, Laura had felt uncomfortable, knowing he was putting on an act for her. She needed to leave him to his own thoughts.

The idea of telling him the truth about her profession had gone clean out of the window. She didn't dare to think of the consequences of telling him the truth about her career now.

However, it had been impossible to sleep and she had lain tossing and turning until the small hours. Finally she had slept a dreamless sleep and awoken to the sounds of voices and activity. Now she looked out of the bedroom window and gasped at the stunning view of the landscape that stretched for miles all around. Her room overlooked the Beaulieu vineyards, and this morning they were a hive of activity.

A dozen or more people were amongst the vines, and while no-one was picking the grapes yet, it was clear that excitement was gathering for the start of the harvest tomorrow.

Dressed in cut-off denims and a strappy top, she went downstairs. The house, too, buzzed with anticipation. There were two French women in the kitchen, the younger one was stocking up the fridge and shelves with fresh meats, fruits, vegetables, cheeses and eggs, while the other was baking bread. They exchanged glances at one another as Laura greeted them. She felt slightly embarrassed, wondering if they assumed she had spent the night with Philippe. The two women continued with their work and their chattering, one checking items off a long shopping list, the other pummelling dough with her fists on the rustic old table. Leaving them to it, Laura wandered outside into the sunshine.

Over at the industrialised part of his land, Philippe's employees were busying themselves with the equipment needed for tomorrow. Some were hosing all the machinery down, and two other men were placing giant tubs strategically at the ends of rows of vines. Heaps of individual baskets stood waiting for volunteers to take and fill, while the sound of the automatic press could be heard from inside one of the buildings, warming up, possibly.

Laura looked around for Philippe and finally spotted him deep in conversation with two of his workforce. She didn't want to interrupt. Clearly there was much to do in readiness for the harvest. Instead, she wandered down to the vines and meandered through the tall rows of plants, lush and heavy with plump, ripe grapes.

The morning was already hot with barely a cloud in the sky — certainly no sign of any approaching hurricane. Laura breathed in the fragrances, delighting in simply being here, being part of this world — Philippe's world. It was going to be hard to leave all this behind, to leave *him* behind. Then, as if her thoughts had conjured him up from nowhere, she jumped as a familiar voice said her name.

'*Bonjour*, Laura. How are you this morning? Did you sleep well?'

She turned and found him gazing down on her. Her heart flipped and she smiled warmly back at him.

'Good morning, Philippe. I'm fine, thanks. How are you?'

'I am very fine also. A happy man!' he said, taking her hand and linking it through his arm. He led her back towards the buildings where his workers were milling around in preparation of the harvest. 'Come, I want to introduce you to everyone.'

Laura went willingly, glad that the melancholy mood that had settled over him last night seemed well and truly lifted. Today he looked ready to take on the world.

She was introduced to the vineyard manager, Claude, a team of growers and, returning to the house, she was officially introduced to the two women in the kitchen who, Philippe explained, were employed as cooks and house-keepers when the need arose.

Laura sensed the two women whispering the instant she and Philippe had walked away. However, Laura found that all his staff were cheerful and welcoming, and she lost count of the number of times she was kissed on hand and cheeks.

'They're all so lovely,' Laura said quietly to Philippe when the introductions were over. 'But what about the grape pickers? Will there be more people coming tomorrow?'

'Ah, *oui*! Tomorrow at daybreak they will come. Claude will register everyone and keep a record of the hours they work so we can pay them accordingly.'

'Do the same people turn up year after year?' she asked, excited by the thought that Lucy Day might actually turn up. If she did it would be wonderful. It would mean Philippe had nothing to do with her disappearance — which she was sure of now anyway.

'Our neighbours from the nearest villages are very loyal,' Philippe said. 'We are expecting them out in full force, and of course we have many gypsies and students who do this purely for the money.'

'I'd love to help. Could I, Philippe?'

His face broke into a wide smile.

'It was my hope that you would. But I warn you, it is hard work.'

'I don't mind that!' she assured him.

'But today,' he continued, linking her hand through his arm once again. 'Today, before the chaos truly begins, I wish to sketch you and paint you, to capture you on canvas.' His eyes sparkled with devilment as he gazed down on her. 'Then I can hold you here for ever.'

Laura didn't dare allow herself to think that his feelings were anything special for her. It was simply his way, she reminded herself. He was no doubt still in love with his dead fiancée, and probably involved with any number of society women — and Melissa, probably. There was no place in his life for anyone as ordinary as her. He was just being flirtatious.

She laughed softly, turning her face aside so he couldn't read the effects his words were having on her emotions.

'But first I have to fetch my sketch pad and pencils,' he announced, patting her hand before disentangling himself from her. 'Meet me amongst the vines, Laura. I shall not be long.'

'Should I change?' she asked, glancing down at her cut-off denims and simple top.

'Later!' he said, striding away. 'For

now, you are perfect.'

She laughed again. Perfect! That was a first, she thought to herself, as he headed back to the house. No-one had ever called her perfect before.

She was chatting to one of the growers when Philippe returned, sketchpad under his arm and his case of pencils in hand. The grower spoke a little English and was keen to practise it. However, Philippe had no time to waste and took her hand, whisking her away with an apology to the other man. He led her into an area rich in vine leaves and fruit. Plump lush bunches of grapes hung heavily on the vines, bending the branches under their weight.

'If you would stand just here, Laura,' he said, gently adjusting the angle of her body and face until he was satisfied. He flicked his pad open to a fresh page and began to sketch, his hand flicking over the white page in light purposeful strokes.

She could see what he was drawing.

She could see an image of herself swiftly emerging on the page. He didn't seem to mind if she chatted, which she did to hide her nervousness. Rather he welcomed it, stopping her at times in mid flow to capture a particular expression which she was unaware of doing.

After the first sketch, he turned to a fresh page, and took her deeper into the vines. He chose another place, another pose and began his work all over again. He sketched for an hour and filled page after page with line drawings of her. Finally he closed the sketch pad and smiled at her.

'That is enough for now. You must be hungry!'

Food had been the last thing on her mind, but now she realised she was a little hungry. Last night's meal was hours ago, and she hadn't had breakfast.

'Starving!' she told him with a laugh.

'Then we shall eat.'

The walked in single file between the

vines, and Laura delighted in admiring his physique as he walked ahead. There was no doubt about it, he was utterly gorgeous. Today he wore denims and a black T-shirt that showed off his broad shoulders and long, lean back. He glanced back over one broad shoulder unexpectedly and caught her looking at him. As she felt her cheeks glow, she was positive she heard him chuckle.

Coming out from the rows of vines, they crossed the lawns and strolled back to the house. Laura made her excuses to go inside to freshen up and find a sun hat.

'Meet me in the garden, Laura,' he said, heading towards the kitchen. 'Would scrambled eggs and crispy bacon be good for you?'

'Would it!' she exclaimed, her stomach rumbling hungrily. 'That would be fantastic!'

He walked away, smiling to himself.

Breakfast, or rather brunch, as it was now mid-morning, was delicious, and they chatted easily as they devoured the eggs, bacon, crusty bread and fresh orange juice.

Afterwards Philippe explained that he had a lot of work to do in preparation for the harvest and so Laura suggested that she took advantage of the hire car and go for a drive.

'You will drive carefully now, Laura,' Philippe fretted, handing her the keys hesitantly. 'We drive on the right here, remember.'

'I'll be fine,' she said, laughing at his facetiousness, but then she saw the serious glint in his eye and knew that he wasn't joking at all. 'Really, Philippe, I'll drive carefully.'

'*Bon*! Enjoy your excursion, and I will see you later.' His hands closed lightly around her upper arms and he placed a light kiss on both cheeks.

Laura climbed into the car tingling from his touch, loving the sensation of his lips against her skin, even though it had been nothing more than the usual French custom. She went to close the door, but he stooped down close to her, causing her heart to lurch. However, there were no more kisses, he simply wanted to help her adjust her seat into position, and ensure she understood all the controls. He eventually stood, and closed the door for her.

'Take care!'

She put the car into gear and gave him a little wave.

'*Au revoir!*'

He remained standing in the driveway, watching her, until she had turned out into the lane and was lost from sight. Her fingertips touched her cheek and, breathing deeply, she was aware that she could still catch the fresh fragrance of him. She kept the windows closed as she drove so that she didn't lose it.

Once away from the house, she found a place to park and consult her map to try and locate the village of Pierry. It proved quite easy and, after driving along country lanes that were flanked on either side by lush vineyards, she found herself eventually approaching the village where Lucy Day lived — if Madame Beaulieu was correct.

After driving through the village once, she back-tracked and found a place to park. Getting out, she took a stroll, enjoying the sights and hoping ridiculously that she might just by chance bump into Lucy Day herself — it wasn't beyond the realms of possibility if the girl really did live here. She even attempted asking around but soon realised her French wasn't good enough to make herself understood by the locals. Eventually she left and drove into Épernay, the main town of the Champagne region, where she spent a few hours being a tourist, and loving every minute of it. By the time she drove back to Champagne de Beaulieu, it was late afternoon, and a large marquee had been erected on the grassy area between the garden and the vines. Quite a number of strangers were strolling around and she saw, too, that a barbecue had been set up that many were making good use of. Laura guessed they were the travellers who had come especially for the harvest and she was pleased to see that Philippe had laid on provisions for them.

She found Philippe in his studio, working on a new picture, as far as she could tell. He stopped immediately when she appeared, giving her no chance this time to stand and admire the great artist at work. Wiping his hands on a cloth, he came towards her, his face lighting up.

'Ah! You are back! I was beginning to worry that you had lost your way.'

For a second she thought he was going to kiss her, and she had an irresistible urge to run into his arms and kiss him, but she remained rooted to the spot, motionless.

'No problems.' She shrugged. 'I had a nice drive around and explored some of the villages.'

Reeling off a few names, she thought she detected a flicker of his eyes when she mentioned Pierry, but he made no comment and so she continued.

'Then I drove into Épernay, parked up and explored the town. It was lovely.'

'That is good. I am glad you have had a good day,' he replied, steering her from the room. 'And what is even better is that now you are home.'

His words struck a chord deep in her heart. Home. It sounded wonderful.

'Now I must shower and change. And I would love to sketch you again, if you do not mind. This time, would you please put on that lovely dress you wore last night and let your hair flow free?'

She was flattered that he wanted to draw her again, but flippantly she responded, 'Well, if you're sure. Aren't you sick of staring at my face yet?'

His eyes softened as he gazed at her.

'How could I ever grow tired of looking at you?'

Her heart thudded. Did he mean it? Or was this his usual patter? Determined not to let him know that his sweet talk was having any effect upon her, she shook her head as if she didn't believe him and laughed.

'Philippe, you could charm the birds from the trees.'

'You think I am joking? You think that I don't mean every word that I say?' His tone was almost as if he was offended, but Laura didn't dare start to believe that he could actually care for her. If she let her guard down and allowed him truly into her heart, she could end up being dreadfully hurt.

She looked steadily into his eyes, trying to read what was in his mind and his heart. What she saw there stunned her. He did care — more than that even. There was love in his eyes.

'Laura, do you think I am merely being flippant — flirtatious?' he repeated earnestly.

She looked swiftly away, her heart beating rapidly.

'I don't know. I don't know you very well.'

'Do you not, Laura?' he murmured. 'You are an intelligent, beautiful young

179

woman. I would not insult you by lying to you.'

She turned aside, knowing this whole relationship was built on a pack of lies — for her part at least. Quietly she murmured, 'Then perhaps you don't know me well enough, Philippe.'

'Tell me about yourself then, Laura,' he pleaded, taking her hands in his. 'Tell me everything there is to know about you.'

She looked up into his face. His expression was intense, deep furrows were etched across his brow. She could just tell him now, blurt out the fact that she was a journalist — the most hated profession in his eyes. It was because of the media that his fiancée had died. They had wrecked his life. Oh, but how could she tell him that she was one of those people? Would he listen long enough for her to convince him of her passion for the truth of a story, that she, too, had no time for scandal and gossip? Would he listen?

Lucy Day

The ringing of Philippe's mobile phone shattered the moment. Or maybe she had been saved by the bell. She wasn't sure, but she stood silently as Philippe took his mobile from his pocket and looked to see who was calling. Apologetically, he said, '*Excusez moi*, Laura. I have to take this call.'

'I'll go and change then,' she said, relieved that the moment had passed. But she would have to tell him. And the sooner the better.

He nodded and spoke into the phone.

'*Bonjour*, Mama.'

Laura left him talking to his mother, her thoughts in turmoil. Unless she had totally misunderstood, Philippe did actually like her. In fact, when she had looked into his eyes, she thought she had seen love shining there. And perhaps if she had dared to drop her guard, he would have seen the love shining back from her own eyes.

She showered, washed her hair and let it dry naturally. Her bedroom windows were open and the warm evening air flowed around her room, bringing in the fragrances from the vines and the sound of birdsong. It was beautiful and she felt truly at home here. The only cloud on the horizon was the fact that she had lied to him. Even the prospect of Philippe having something to do with the disappearance of Lucy Day had paled to insignificance now. He was innocent of that, Laura was positive. But what she had to do now was tell him the truth.

A half hour later she returned downstairs. Philippe was in the kitchen putting something in the oven. There was no sign of the two French cooks. His gaze swept appreciatively over her as she walked in.

'Ah! You look so beautiful, Laura. That is the look I wish to capture now.'

Her nerves were stretched tight. Words, explanations, excuses were swirling round and around in her head. Surely he would listen, surely he would understand. She took a deep breath.

'Philippe, I need to — ' but he picked up his sketchpad and pencils from the table and swept her up in his excitement of the moment.

'This light, Laura,' he said, taking her outside. 'This light as the sun is low in the sky, this is what I want to capture. I want to see how the golden glow lights up your hair and your skin. We must work quickly before it changes.'

There was no time to talk and she found herself running with him, hand in hand across the lawns ignoring the startled glances of the travellers and students milling around. They ran down to where the vines stood in their regimented rows. Philippe turned her aside from them, so that they were merely distant background with a huge red sun sinking into the horizon, sweeping the land with its brilliance.

He sketched frantically, as if he was racing against time, adding colour, holding different coloured pencils between his fingers, switching from one to the other, colour over colour, smudging the shades with his fingertips. He didn't speak to her, but murmured to himself, like he was caught up in some fever that would only be dowsed when the work was done.

The sun slowly set. Philippe worked on, moving around his subject now, rather than adjusting her stance. Laura stood silently, motionless, watching him, encased in the magic of this great artist at work. Seeing the passion he had for his creations. And above all else, she was aware of one thing. She was desperately in love with him.

Only when the sun had finally disappeared beyond the horizon and the final streaks of gold and red had sunk, leaving the sky a pale dove grey, did Philippe finally close his sketchpad and sink to his knees.

Laura stepped towards him. He

looked exhausted. His head hung low, his shoulders were hunched and he looked totally drained. She stood close to him, her hand moving to touch the top of his head, her trembling fingertips stroking his hair, loving the feel of that soft silkiness.

Then his hands reached up to her, bringing her closer to him, so that his face was buried against her midriff. Laura caught her breath, her fingers tangling deeper now into his hair, stroking it back from his face.

He drew her down until she, too, was kneeling on the cold grass, facing him, and he looked into her eyes. Beyond the look of exhaustion, she saw elation, and she saw love.

Without a word, he kissed her. It was a kiss so tender that Laura wanted to cry with happiness. It was a kiss that told her, if she hadn't already realised it, that he loved her. It was a kiss that promised so much more.

When it ended, he smiled at her, then holding her hands, drew her to her feet.

185

'Let us go inside and eat,' he said simply.

Laura nodded, and linked her fingers between his. They walked in silence back to the house — a comfortable, easy silence. There was no need for words. The moment was perfect. It was a moment she would remember for ever.

It was the quietest meal they had shared together — neither had anything to say. The kiss and all it revealed had created a turning point. A point of no return. Both of them knew it and accepted it willingly.

The truth about her career would resolve itself, she was sure. Their love would fade the problem into insignificance.

Another telephone call just as they were finishing dessert marred the glorious mood.

'*Excusez moi*, Laura, I must answer this. *Bonsoir*, Melissa.'

Laura was glad to see that he made no move to take the call in private, and

186

as he talked into his phone he reached across the table and took her hand. He spoke in French to his Girl Friday and, despite her good intentions, Laura reluctantly found herself trying to decipher what was being said. When he finally hung up, it was with a sigh.

'There is a problem, Laura. Melissa is unable to drive into Paris to collect my mother this evening. She has family commitments. She is expecting a visitor. I shall have to go myself.' He looked utterly dejected. 'I am sorry to have to leave you.'

'That's fine, Philippe. Do what you have to. I'm quite tired anyway. I'll just go to bed. I imagine it's an early start in the morning.'

He brought her hand to his lips.

'At first light. I can't wait to introduce you to Mama. She will love you.'

Laura waved goodbye to him from the front steps, watching his car's tail lights until they had curled out on to the lane and disappeared. She returned indoors and busied herself clearing away the dinner dishes and tidying the kitchen, feeling uncannily like this was home — as if she truly belonged here.

Before going up to bed, she wickedly had the urge to peep into Philippe's studio and take a little peek at the painting he was doing of her. Despite promising that she wouldn't look, the prospect was too irresistible, and he would never know.

She crept softly into his studio, and even though there was no-one else at home, she felt the need to be quiet. Flicking on the light, she stood for a moment in the room, breathing in the smells of paints and oils, these fragrances that were part of Philippe's world — a vital part of his world.

The canvas he had been working on was far from finished, but it was of her, and she was startled at how good he had made her look. She was quite sure she wasn't that pretty. Then another painting caught her eye, leaning against the wall, a cloth only half covering it.

Recognising the features in this half-sketched, half-painted work, she lifted the cloth and stared at her own face again. He had started the picture then maybe grown tired of it, cast it aside. It wasn't the only one. As she explored the studio she found another two canvasses which had been started and then discarded.

The discoveries puzzled her. He had said that he tried to see what worked and what didn't. Well, so far, he wasn't happy with any of the pictures he had painted of her. Maybe tonight's colouring would be more successful.

Eventually she went to bed, but there were too many thoughts spinning round in her head to allow her to sleep. But they were, in the main, happy thoughts. The one tiny cloud on the horizon was the worry of how Philippe would take the news that she was a journalist. But surely, if he loved her, that wouldn't make such a difference now.

She finally slept and dreamed of blue skies over a world of lush vines. Then in her dream a small white cloud floated into view, followed closely by rolling black thunderclouds that burst and flooded the earth in torrential rain, sweeping the grapes from the vines and washing them away in a flood of misery.

★ ★ ★

Laura's dream was the first thing she recalled as she opened her eyes, and she jumped out of bed to look at the weather through her window, terrified in case the storm had come in the night and destroyed a year's work. She heaved a huge sigh of relief as she looked out at a silvery blue sky and a host of people, preparing for the busy day ahead.

She dressed in her cut-off denims again and added a light shirt over a vest top, knowing she would have to keep covered if she wasn't to get sunburned. She tied her hair up in a ponytail and ran downstairs, eager to see Philippe again. The smell of freshly baked bread filled the house and Laura wasn't surprised to find the two cooks in the kitchen, preparing a breakfast fit to feed an army.

Outside, the vineyard was awash with people — gypsies, students, some that she recognised from the night before, others that were new to her. Claude, the vineyard manager, was seated at a table near the top of the drive with an open ledger and pen, registering those who had come to help with the harvest. Watching the procedure, Laura saw that after he had taken their particulars, another of Philippe's workers took small groups of people towards the vines, provided them with a basket and allocated particular rows of vines for them to work on.

It all seemed to be running like clockwork, and it was clear that this was a procedure that they had undertaken for many, many years.

The atmosphere buzzed with joviality and excitement and Laura was instantly caught up in the ambience. Long trestle tables had been set up on the grass near the marquee on which stood pitchers of water, wine and juice, and judging by the amount of food being prepared indoors, Laura guessed that those tables would also soon be groaning under the weight of breakfast.

She caught sight of Philippe then, talking with a small crowd of newcomers. Laura hung back until he was free and ran over to him. His face lit up as he saw her and she ran joyfully into his arms. His kiss was light on her lips and his hands stroked the curve of her back, moulding her to him, gazing down at her with a look that made her dizzy.

'It is wonderful to see you, Laura,' he murmured, stroking a strand of hair back from her eyes. 'I have missed you.'

'I've missed you, too, Philippe,' she said softly, linking her arms around his neck, allowing her fingers to stray into the softness of his hair.

He chuckled to himself, as if he knew he was being ridiculous.

'It is crazy, but you only have to be

out of my sight for a minute and I am missing you.' His arms tightened around her. 'This is where you belong, Laura. Close to me.'

Raymond, the cellar master, interrupted. He looked utterly apologetic at breaking into the moment, but Philippe spoke to him in French, seeming to assure him that it was fine. Laura stepped aside, allowing the two men to talk. By the rapidity of the conversation, Laura gathered that Philippe's presence was needed elsewhere.

He turned to her, a rueful smile on his lips.

'I have to leave you, Laura. I am needed. There is much I am needed to do.'

'I want to help. What shall I do?' she asked eagerly.

His smile broadened. 'It is hard work, but if you wish to help I am happy. Please, talk to Claude and he will tell you what to do. Sadly, I may not see very much of you today until the sun goes down.'

'I'll look forward to seeing you later then,' she murmured shyly, lowering her eyes.

He cupped her chin between two fingers, bringing her face up to meet his.

'Until tonight, then.' He placed another kiss on her lips.

'I can't wait!' she murmured as he released her.

'Do not work too hard!' he called, walking away towards the grape press buildings with Raymond.

She waved and skipped across the grass and up the drive to where Claude sat at his table near the entrance. He was talking to another new arrival, obviously an old friend, because the two stood chatting amicably for some time. Laura waited patiently, gazing around. Idly she glanced down at the register in the ledger, wondering what information she would have to give. She didn't want paying for her work, she simply wanted to know where she should start.

She saw the list of names of people already here and a horrible thought struck her. Should she give her name as Laura Stevens — the name Philippe knew her by, or her real name, Laura Kane? She made up her mind there and then to begin telling the truth and take the consequences.

As the two men chattered on, her gaze swept down the list of names. Her knees buckled as she spotted the name *Lucy Day*. For a second she couldn't believe her eyes. But there it was, as clear as day, halfway down the page.

Lucy Day was here! Her long, long search, the countless newspaper reports and appeals had ended here, in Philippe Beaulieu's vineyards. She could hardly believe it. And best of all, it meant that Philippe was not some dastardly kidnapper. She laughed at herself. She had never truly thought that anyway. But at least now she was doubly sure — and she could hardly wait to meet Lucy Day for herself.

Claude and his friend finally wound

up their conversation and shook hands. The newcomer picked up a basket and sauntered, whistling, down the drive towards the vines. Claude sat back down at the table and smiled up at Laura.

'Ah, *bonjour*, Laura. You wish to pick grapes?'

'Yes, I do, please!'

He wrote her name on the sheet, then glanced at her again.

'Remind me of your last name, *mademoiselle*. It has slipped my mind.'

She took a deep breath, hoping that Philippe wouldn't look down this list before she had a chance to tell him the truth. She hesitated. Philippe needed to know first. Her decision of a minute ago to sign in as Laura Kane suddenly worried her. She couldn't risk Phillipe just coming across it in his ledger. Determined that this would be the last fib, she said. 'Stevens, Laura Stevens.'

'Ah, *oui*.' He nodded, remembering. '*Merci!*' He jotted it down and indicated that she took a basket and follow the man he had just been talking to.

With a brief smile, Laura picked up a basket and ran down the drive to catch up with Claude's old friend.

He spoke no English, but he was pleasant and showed her exactly how to pick the fruit so that it wasn't damaged. She discovered that it was indeed hard work. Her fingers weren't used to plucking the grapes from their branches, and she soon realised she was not the fastest picker along her row. In fact, she was the slowest. Nevertheless, after filling her first basket and depositing it in the big container at the end of the row, she felt amazingly pleased and satisfied with her humble effort.

Helping Philippe, the man she loved, with his harvest filled her with a sense of joy. It was a joy made even better now that she knew Lucy Day was here somewhere. She couldn't wait to meet her, and each time she walked along to the end of the row with her full basket, she kept her eyes peeled for sight of the auburn-haired teenager with the musical stave tattoo on her shoulder.

There was no sign of Lucy, but Laura did spot Melissa. Dressed in shorts, a tiny vest and floppy straw hat, she looked any man's ideal woman, and Laura wondered if Philippe had ever painted her.

Irritated with herself for being unable to stop these ridiculous feelings of jealousy, Laura tried to push such thoughts out of her head.

She had been working for a couple of hours, and the big tub had twice been hauled back to the press by a small tractor, when a hand bell rang out across the fields.

'What's that?' she asked the friendly Frenchman working close by.

'Ah! *Petit dejeuner! Avez-vous faim?*' He rubbed his tummy to indicate that it was time for breakfast.

'*Oui! Oui!*' Laura nodded, placing her basket on the ground, and following him and the others pickers out on to the grassy area where breakfast was being served. The trestle tables were filled with croissants, cold meats, hard boiled eggs, crusty fresh bread and butter, cheeses and fruit.

She squeezed between two Eastern European women and poured herself a glass of orange juice, and put some food on a plate. The whole workforce had stopped for a well-earned meal so, finding a grassy spot to sit, Laura sat cross-legged to enjoy her *petit dejeuner*. As she ate she kept a keen lookout for Lucy Day.

She was surprised when Melissa came and sat down beside her. Close to, Laura could see that she was without make-up and her hair was pinned untidily under her hat. So different from when dressed for her chauffeur's job.

'Are you enjoying the harvest, Laura?' Melissa asked in her exquisite Parisian accent.

'Oh, yes, it's wonderful — hard work but wonderful.'

The other woman tucked into a

chunk of crusty bread.

'This is the best time of the year, but also the most worrying time. At least until we have harvested all the grapes.'

'There's a good turn out of helpers,' Laura ventured. 'I was hoping to find an English girl who might be here — Lucy Day. Do you know her?'

Melissa shrugged.

'No, I don't know her.'

'Oh! I thought I heard you mention her name yesterday.'

She remained looking blank.

'I do not think so.'

Laura ventured on relentlessly.

'When you were talking to Philippe. Didn't I hear you mention Lucy Day?'

'No. You are mistaken.' Her face broke into a huge smile then as she focused on someone heading their way.

Laura glanced up to see a young man in shorts and T-shirt with spiky hair and a deep tan. He had eyes only for Melissa, and flopped down beside her, but not before placing a kiss on both cheeks and her lips.

'Laura, this is my fiancé,' Melissa introduced the young man. 'Lucas, this is Laura Stevens, Philippe's friend.'

He took Laura's hand, smiling warmly. '*Enchanté*, Laura.'

'Perhaps,' Melissa continued, 'you heard me saying that Lucas was arriving one day this week.'

'I must have,' Laura admitted, delighted to know that Melissa wasn't the threat that she thought she was. And perhaps she had heard incorrectly.

After eating a good breakfast, Laura left Melissa and Lucas alone to see if she could find the elusive Lucy Day. Most of the pickers were wearing sun hats, shielding their faces, but Laura meandered around the crowd of people, searching for that familiar face, although she wondered if she would actually recognise the girl. It had been a whole year, and she might have changed a lot from the photographs she'd put in her newspaper appeals. She could have changed her hair colour, anything.

Then, suddenly, she spotted a girl sitting on the grass, eating and talking to a small group of people. She wore a thin strapped T-shirt, and the tattoo on her left shoulder was of a musical stave and three notes. The teenager was chatting in French, but as Laura wandered discreetly nearer she realised it wasn't the same accent as the others spoke, there was something very English about her phrases and pronunciation.

Laura moved to stand in front of her, and looked down at her face. Instantly recognising the face of the young girl about whom she had written appeal after appeal in her local paper for more than a year. At last, there she was. The shock of seeing her in person rather than a faded old photograph made her catch her breath.

The girl looked happy and seemed to glow with health, as if life here was agreeing with her, but Laura couldn't help thinking back to the interviews she'd conducted with the girl's mother and stepfather, and how distraught they had been when she'd vanished.

Laura knew that the mother and stepfather had now split up, perhaps because of the stress over the missing girl, and Laura desperately wanted to ask this teenager if she had ever stopped to ask herself how her disappearance was affecting the ones she'd left behind. There had never been so much as a postcard or telephone call.

Looking at her now, it struck Laura as being a selfish thing to do — but, of course, she didn't know what she was running from.

Lucy Day obviously sensed that Laura was now staring at her, and stopped her chatter to look up.

'Lucy Day?' Laura asked, smiling.

Lucy Day dropped the plate of food she was holding and the colour drained instantly from her face.

'Lucy?' Laura repeated, 'I'm Laura Kane, I . . . '

With a cry, the teenager jumped to her feet and fled, leaving everyone staring, first at the girl racing across the lawn towards the drive — and then at Laura. The faces that stared at her were angry and accusing.

'I'm sorry. I didn't mean to frighten her.'

A young man from the group she had been talking to threw down his napkin and got to his feet.

'*Vous l'anglais!*' he spat, as if that explained everything. Then he raced after the receding figure of Lucy Day.

Laura turned helplessly to everyone else.

'I'm sorry. I know her from back in England, that's all. I didn't mean to upset her.'

The others didn't say a word, just continued staring at her with harsh accusing expressions on their faces.

'I need to speak to her.' Laura turned, and without another word, ran after them both.

While Lucy had already disappeared out of the gates, Laura spotted the young man going left, so she followed in his footsteps, running as fast as she could, sweating in the heat and breathing hard. But she couldn't just leave it like this. Whatever Lucy Day had run away from, she was obviously still terrified that it would catch up with her. Laura had to reassure her that her secret life was safe with her. She would respect her privacy and wouldn't breathe a word to anyone, let alone report on it.

It must have been something dreadful to make a young teenager leave her home and friends without a word. Whatever it was, Laura needed to assure her she had nothing to fear from her.

She had a stitch in her side as she ran along the lane and was relieved when she spotted two figures hunched together beside a gate, catching their breath. The young man seemed to be comforting the distraught teenager.

Laura approached them slowly, holding her side.

Lucy Day spotted her, and made

another frantic sprint. Laura called out.

'Please! I only want to speak to you. You've nothing to be frightened of!'

The young man grabbed hold of Lucy's arms, and Laura recognised the gestures that seemed to say she couldn't keep running, that she should wait and hear what was to be said.

Glad to be able to walk the last few hundred metres, Laura took the opportunity to get her breath back. The couple stood there, arms around each other, and Laura instantly saw how protective the young man was to her.

'I'm sorry I frightened you, Lucy,' Laura said, as she got closer.

'Who are you?' the young Frenchman demanded, placing himself between them both.

Laura thought it was utterly gallant of him and she couldn't help but smile.

'My name is Laura Kane. I'm a reporter on the 'Westgate Evening Standard' — your home town paper, Lucy.'

'What do you want?' Lucy snapped,

clutching the young man's arm for protection.

'I don't want anything,' Laura said softly, hating herself for inflicting such fear on another human being.

'Who sent you? Did *he* send you?' The word 'he' came out as something vile.

'No-one has sent me, Lucy. Please, don't be frightened. I'm not going to tell anyone back home that you're here. Your new life here is safe — if that's what you want,' Laura told the girl.

'I'm never going back there,' she cried, shaking her head wildly.

'No-one is asking you to,' Laura said gently, beginning to guess what she had run away from.

'I'm just glad that you are all right — and alive,' Laura explained. 'Your disappearance caused such concerns in our little town, Lucy. Although it was my job to report the story, I was actually worried about you. I didn't let the story drop. It wasn't right that a teenager could vanish and people should forget.'

Lucy's eyes filled with tears.

'I wanted to tell her I was safe, but she'd have told him. She was under his thumb, she worshipped him. She didn't believe me when I told her I'd seen him with another woman. She called me a liar. She took his word against mine.'

'Well, they aren't together now,' Laura informed her, and saw Lucy reel in surprise. 'That made news, too — tragic parents split due to stress over missing daughter.'

'He wasn't my real father!' Lucy said angrily.

'Your mother is on her own now, Lucy, and no doubt still praying that one day she will learn what has happened to her little girl.'

Tears suddenly coursed down Lucy's cheeks. The young man held her sobbing against his chest.

'That's all I have to say,' Laura murmured, turning away. 'I won't tell on you. Your secret is safe — and that's a promise. I won't say anything to anyone about finding you, not even to your mother if I should bump into her in the street. I do sometimes, it's a small town — well, you know that.'

'How is she?' Lucy sniffed.

'Sad,' Laura murmured. 'She's very sad.'

'And he's definitely not with her?'

'He doesn't even live in our town anymore, Lucy,' Laura assured her. 'He moved away four or five months ago.'

Nervously, Lucy asked, 'Do you think my mum will forgive me for running away? Will she want to hear from me, do you think?'

'Oh, Lucy, it's all she wants.'

Lucy looked into her young man's eyes, and Laura saw the look that passed between them. She saw the decision that Lucy came to that very moment. And while she didn't say another word, she sensed that very soon Lucy's mother would have a welcome phone call from someone very special. Laura turned and walked away.

'Laura Kane!'

She glanced back to find Lucy running towards her. Reaching her the girl planted a kiss on her cheek.

'Thank you for not giving up on me.'

Laura could feel tears pricking her own eyes and she shrugged them brusquely away.

'Oh, you know us hard-nosed reporters, once we get the bit between our teeth, there's no letting go!'

'Thank goodness for that.' Lucy smiled.

Laura walked back to Philippe's house feeling like she was walking on air.

The Truth

Turning through the wrought-iron gates of Champagne de Beaulieu, Laura felt like dancing. She wondered whether she would be able to tell Philippe her joy at finding Lucy. Maybe this could illustrate why she loved her job so much. It was at times like this, when a happy conclusion was reached, that made everything worthwhile.

Once thing was for sure, though, she wouldn't be writing about it. It was finished now. She would honour her promise not to breathe a word and certainly not to write a word.

Walking up the drive, she saw that everyone was back amongst the vines, picking grapes. The tractor was lugging another big tub full of grapes and tipping them into the press and the place buzzed with activity.

As she passed by Philippe's house,

she spotted a figure emerging from the garden. A woman dressed in a pretty cotton sundress, sun hat and sunglasses, but there was no mistaking Philippe's mother by the sheer elegance that she exuded in her style and grace of movement. In contrast to her own jeans and shirt, with her hair dishevelled from running, Laura suddenly realised that she and Philippe were from two very different worlds.

She didn't know whether Madame Beaulieu would remember her from the night of the exhibition, or indeed whether Philippe had even mentioned that he had a house guest. Unsure whether to speak first or to just get back to her job grape picking, Laura smiled and went to walk by. However, Madame Beaulieu made the decision for her.

'Laura!' she said, raising a hand in a little wave.

Laura stopped in her tracks. Uncertainly, she murmured, '*Bonjour*, Madame Beaulieu.'

'Ah, I thought it was you.' The older woman smiled extending her hand, and then kissed Laura on both cheeks. 'I am Margot Beaulieu, Philippe's mother. We met at the exhibition in Paris.'

'Yes, we did,' Laura agreed, surprised that she'd remembered.

'My son said you were staying for a day or two. How nice to meet you.'

'It's nice to see you again, too, Madame.'

Madame Beaulieu glanced down at Laura's hands, stained by juice.

'You are helping with the harvest, I see. Are you enjoying yourself?'

'Yes, it's a wonderful experience,' Laura said, feeling slightly grubby in comparison with the older woman's elegant attire.

'I am glad you are having a pleasant time,' Madame Beaulieu said, removing her sunglasses, as if to get a better look at her. 'And has Philippe been looking after you?'

There was something not quite right, Laura suddenly sensed. Something in

213

the way she was speaking to her, as if she was slightly suspicious, disapproving even. Laura's responses became equally as unyielding.

'Yes, he's been very hospitable.'

'Naturally, yes. But I gather you and he are becoming close.'

Laura felt herself blush.

'I . . . I don't know . . . '

Madame Beaulieu continued to look oddly at her.

'I have to say, I am a little surprised.'

Laura stared at her.

'Surprised? Why?'

Madame Beaulieu raised her eyebrows and all but looked down her nose at her.

'Well, I would have thought that was obvious.'

Laura felt herself curl up and die. The division between Philippe and her suddenly opened like a chasm. Philippe, wealthy with his glamorous lifestyle and beautiful friends, and her, an ordinary unglamorous Plain Jane! She could see that was what she was thinking. What's my rich, eligible, handsome son doing with a Plain Jane like this?

Colour scorched Laura's cheeks. She couldn't believe that with all her elegance, Madame Beaulieu could be so cutting. It wasn't what she'd expected from Philippe's mother and it hurt.

Somehow Laura found her voice.

'He doesn't seem to mind.'

Madame Beaulieu shook her head.

'Well, that amazes me. It truly amazes me.'

'Would you excuse me, Madame.' Laura made her excuses, as a lump lodged itself in her throat. 'There's someone I need to speak to.'

Tears were pricking her eyes as she hurried away to lose herself amongst the vines. Yes, she was well aware that she was way out of Philippe Beaulieu's league, but to be reminded in so brutal a manner was too unkind.

'Laura!' Madame Beaulieu called after her.

Laura pretended not to have heard.

She was working, head down, picking grapes for all she was worth when she heard her name being called again. She recognised Philippe's voice immediately. Glancing up she spotted him easing his way between the rows of vines, stepping around the various workers without so much as a word to them, his blue eyes fixed intently upon her.

'Laura?' he murmured, stooping slightly to look directly into her eyes. 'You are upset. My mother came to fetch me. She said you ran off looking like you were about to cry. What has happened? Who has upset you?'

'It's nothing, no-one,' she murmured stiffly, determined not to give way to more tears.

'Please tell me,' he pleaded, relieving her of her basket, and leading her out from the vines. 'You do not cry for nothing.'

'I can't say. It's nothing, really.'

He wasn't going to take no for an

216

answer, however.

'Has one of the pickers upset you?'

'No, the people are lovely.'

'Then who?' he asked, dumbfounded. 'One minute you are talking to my mother, and then you run away in tears.'

Her silence told him and his eyebrows shot up.

'My mother! She upset you?' He sounded as if he just couldn't believe it.

She looked away, feeling foolish.

'It doesn't matter, really.'

'Yes it matters,' he stated, placing an arm around her shoulders and walking her back towards the house. 'It matters greatly!'

'Oh, Philippe, I don't want to cause any trouble. It was nothing and I'm over-reacting.'

'Laura, just tell me, please.'

She heaved a sigh.

'I feel like I'm telling tales. She . . . she said that she was surprised that you'd been hospitable to me and when I asked why, she said it was obvious.'

He looked puzzled.

'I do not understand. Come, we shall go and ask her what she meant by that.'

Laura dug in her heels.

'No, don't! I know what she meant, and it makes me feel such a fool. She meant that I wasn't good enough for you, that I wasn't like the other rich, beautiful and glamorous women you're usually seen with.'

He laughed. Throwing back his dark head, he roared as if it was the funniest thing he'd ever heard. When he'd finished laughing, he smiled lovingly at her.

'Ah, my love, she could not have meant that. You have misunderstood. Come, we will sort this out.'

'No, Philippe, I don't want to be confrontational. If she doesn't think I'm good enough for you, that's her opinion and she's entitled to it. It will embarrass her as well as me if we say anything.'

His response was simply to squeeze her hand reassuringly and to continue walking back up to the house to where his mother was standing, waiting and watching them, her hands clasped together anxiously.

Madame Beaulieu's blue-grey eyes were full of concern as she stepped towards them, taking Laura's hands in hers. 'My dear, what did I say?' She glanced anxiously at her son. 'I have upset her, Philippe, I am so sorry. I don't know why my words have offended you, Laura.'

Philippe remained with his arm around Laura's shoulders, his fingers caressing her overheated skin.

'Mama, you do not usually put your foot in it — to coin an English phrase — but I fear you have this time. Laura was given the opinion that she is not good enough for me. That she is not as glamorous as the other women I date. What have you to say about that, Mama?'

Madame Beaulieu clasped her hands over her mouth.

'That is not what I meant at all.' She squeezed Laura's hands earnestly. 'You are beautiful — not like the women who chase him at all. And that is a good thing, believe me! I meant I was amazed that my son invited you here to stay, because you are a journalist. And he normally has no time for journalists. But clearly you, my dear, have . . . '

Laura heard no more, the rest of Madame Beaulieu's words faded into insignificance as a cold clammy sensation swept up from her feet to her head. No! She wanted to scream. This wasn't how he was to find out about her true profession. Her head swam. She ought to have told him. She had left it too late.

Philippe's hand was still on her shoulder, and she heard him laugh, as if that was the most ridiculous thing he'd ever heard. Then quizzically he said, 'Laura's not a journalist, Mama. Heaven forbid! No, she sells shoes.'

'*Alors! Non*, Philippe. She is a reporter. I arranged her press pass to the exhibition, did I not, Laura? It is Laura Kane from the 'Westgate Evening Standard'.'

'You are mistaken, Mama,' Philippe interrupted, looking relieved. 'Her name is Laura Stevens. You are mixing her up with some other person.'

'Am I? Oh, then I apologise.'

'No,' Laura murmured, feeling icy cold. The word seemed to hang in the mid-air, sealing her fate. 'No. I'm the one who should be apologising.'

Philippe's hand slipped from her shoulder and she began to tremble. He looked at her with such a strange look that she wanted to weep. Disbelief at first, then horror and then a look so full of anguish that he appeared to be about to cry out in pain.

In the blinking of an eye his expression had settled into that cold, fierce look he reserved for people in her profession.

'Go on, Laura,' he murmured coldly. 'What have you to say?'

Her throat became parched, and her heart began thumping so painfully against her ribcage she started to feel faint. Somehow, she stood her ground.

'Your mother is right. My real name is Laura Kane and I'm a journalist with the 'Westgate Evening Standard', which is a reputable . . . ' She heard the sharp intake of his breath and he jerked away from her so sharply it was as if she'd got the plague. 'Philippe, please hear me out. I was here to — '

'Spy on me!' he exploded. 'Seeing what dirt you could find?'

'No!' she cried. 'Of course not, I was looking for someone. A girl who went missing a year ago and turned up in one of your paintings.'

'And you could not have simply asked me about her?' he uttered, his eyes narrowing as if he was in agony.

'I tried, but what you said made me think you were covering something up.'

'So you fabricated an identity and tricked your way into my home?' His eyes met hers, harsh and tortured. 'You lied to me, Laura. You lied to me over and over again.' His voice broke and he turned away.

'Philippe!' Laura begged, clutching

his arm, trying to make him understand. 'Please, listen to me. Hear me
out, please!'

He swung round on her, angrily
dislodging her hands from his arm.

'You are a good liar, Laura Kane.
As I have always said, journalists are
very good at lying. They could not tell
the truth if their lives depended upon
it.'

'No, that's not true, Philippe!'

But he stormed away, his fury barely
contained within his rigid frame. Laura
went to run after him, but his mother
caught her arm.

'Leave him for a while,' she said
firmly. 'Once his anger has subsided he
might listen to what you have to say.'

'I didn't mean to trick him, Madame
Beaulieu,' Laura cried, her head spinning. 'And it certainly wasn't to spy on
him. I was never going to write about
him. In fact, I'd never even heard of
him until I saw that painting in an art
brochure at work. He'd painted a girl in
one of his pictures who had gone

missing from my town. I wanted to try and find her.'

'Well, that is not so terrible,' Madame Beaulieu said kindly.

'But he's right,' Laura uttered, gazing after him, tears flooding down her cheeks. 'I should have told him from the start who I was and why I was here. But I thought he might have been implicated in her disappearance, so I didn't.'

Madame Beaulieu's eyebrows shot up.

'You thought Philippe might have kidnapped this girl?'

She nodded, wiping her eyes with the palm of her hands.

'*Alors!*' The older woman gasped.

'I know it's ridiculous. I can see that now, and anyway I've found her.'

'Well, that is something,' Madame Beaulieu murmured, her austere expression softening.

'Please believe me, Madame, it was never my intention to write about him. I was just trying to trace Lucy Day, but when I saw how Philippe dealt with those reporters at the exhibition, I thought he'd have no time for me, so I pretended I was just interested in the paintings. I didn't force my way into his life. He practically railroaded me into coming here!'

A small smile twitched at the corners of the older woman's mouth.

'Did he?'

'He sent his car to my hotel. His driver, Melissa, wouldn't take no for an answer. So I came. I thought I might learn what had happened to the girl in his picture. I wanted to tell him,' Laura babbled on. 'I was going to tell him if I could find the right moment.'

'*Ma chérie*, there could never be a right moment if you had already lied about yourself and your reasons for being here,' Madame Beaulieu said sternly. 'He has strong reasons for hating the media. They have not been kind to him over the years. His life has been torn into shreds on more than one occasion because of the stories they have printed about him.'

'Yes, he told me,' Laura murmured. 'And that only made it harder to find the moment to tell him the truth, and all the while we were . . . we were . . . '

'Falling in love?'

Laura drew up her shoulders and let them fall.

'Well, he doesn't love me now, that's for sure. He hates me.'

Madame Beaulieu's expression softened.

'Come inside, Laura. Wash your face and we will talk.'

'You're very kind, thank you.'

Madame Beaulieu touched Laura's elbow.

'Come.'

Laura walked beside Philippe's mother back to the house, looking across to the buildings, hoping to catch sight of Philippe, but he was nowhere to be seen. Her heart ached. Such a short time ago she was part of Philippe's harvest — part of his world. How swiftly that happiness had dissolved to nothing but pain.

In the bathroom she washed her tear-stained face and brushed her hair, but nothing would wipe away the look of abject misery from her face as she stared at her reflection in the mirror. There was nothing left now except to pack her case and leave. Philippe wouldn't want her anywhere near him now.

Folding the dress she wore last night, she pressed the soft fabric to her face, recalling how Philippe, on his knees, had held her close to him. Tears welled up in her eyes again and she collapsed on to the bed, burying her face in her pillow to muffle her sobs of misery.

Eventually someone tapped her door and her heart lurched, her hopes soaring. But it was Madame Beaulieu's voice that softly called her name. Her hopes plummeted into the ground.

'Laura? Are you all right?'

'Yes,' she croaked, then cleared her throat and said a little more confidently. 'Yes, I'm fine. I'll be down in a minute.'

'I have made a pot of tea. It is the

English answer to all problems, is it not?'

'Yes, so they say,' Laura uttered, trying to pull herself together.

'Please join me in the sitting-room when you are ready.'

Attempting to cover her red-rimmed eyes with a little make-up in an effort to look presentable, Laura went downstairs with a heavy heart.

Madame Beaulieu had made an effort and the tea did a little to revive her spirits. For some minutes the older woman said nothing, simply sipped from her china tea cup and watched Laura with those sharp blue-grey eyes of hers. After a while she said softly, 'Tell me about yourself, Laura, and your work, and this strange story about the girl in one of Philippe's paintings.'

With a sigh, and trying hard not to dwell on the fact that she might well never see Philippe again, she explained to his mother about her life and her job, and, of course, about Lucy Day.

Madame Beaulieu listened without

interrupting, occasionally filling up their tea cups and nodding her dark head.

For Laura it was a huge relief to actually talk about her job at last, and as she talked, despite her unhappiness over Philippe, there was no hiding her enthusiasm for her profession.

She must have talked for an hour at least, even recapping on how Philippe had taken her to dinner after the exhibition, and re-living the car at the hotel incident which Madame Beaulieu seemed to find quite amusing. Laura smiled at his mother's reaction. It was the moment Philippe chose to appear.

He took one step into the room and stopped. His eyes, blazing with fury, locked on to Laura. Her smile vanished as he growled, 'You are still here!'

Laura's cheeks burned scarlet and she jumped to her feet.

'I'll get my things.'

'Good!' he said, folding his arms and glowering at her.

'Philippe!' Madame Beaulieu snapped.

'Laura is my guest now, and we are having a cup of tea and a pleasant conversation.'

'Ha!' he exclaimed, tossing his head back. 'Be warned, Mama. What she says may not necessarily be the truth.'

Laura gasped.

'I shall be the judge of that,' the older woman said calmly. 'Now, is there a problem? Did you want me?'

'Nothing that can't wait,' he replied, giving Laura the iciest of looks as he added, 'The hire car is at your disposal. You may use it until the end of your vacation and then leave it at the airport.'

Laura wanted to tell him he could keep his hire car, but she realised that she would need some mode of transport to get back to Paris. Right at this minute she was too upset to think straight. So she answered simply, 'Thank you.'

He seemed to hesitate for the briefest moment, as if he had expected some argument from her, or he had something on the tip of his tongue, but he swung away without another word, striding out of the room, closing the door behind him with a resounding snap.

Laura stood trembling, feeling as if her heart was splintering into tiny irreparable pieces. What had happened to the lovely man who made her smile and laugh? Where was the man who had held her in his arms just a few short hours ago?

'I apologise for my son, Laura,' Madame Beaulieu said, sounding quite shocked. 'That is most unlike him.'

'He's angry,' Laura breathed.

'I have seen him angry,' she said, frowning. 'This is something else.'

Laura somehow kept her chin up.

'Thank you for the tea, and for listening. I'd better get my things now and go.'

Philippe's mother got to her feet.

'This is so unfortunate, Laura. What are your plans now?'

Laura breathed deeply before attempting to speak.

'I'm not sure. To be honest, I don't have any plans. Things have changed so quickly.' She tried to rally her thoughts. 'Probably I'll go back to Paris and do some sight-seeing. My flight home isn't for another four days.'

Madame Beaulieu regarded Laura sympathetically.

'It worries me that you will be driving when you are so upset. That troubles me greatly.'

Laura wondered whether she was thinking about Philippe's fiancée, who drove off after a huge argument and died in a car crash. Clearly that thought hadn't troubled Philippe, however. He couldn't wait to get rid of her.

'I'll be fine, Madame. Philippe hates me, and I can understand why.'

'Perhaps,' she murmured. 'But I would not like you driving away from here in a distressed state of mind. You must stay, at least for tonight. Sleep on what has happened, and make your decisions tomorrow.'

Laura shook her head.

'I don't think Philippe is going to like that very much.'

'Then that is too bad,' Madame Beaulieu dismissed with a wave of her arm. 'You are now my guest, Laura, and I insist that you stay until tomorrow.'

'He's going to be furious,' Laura uttered.

'Perhaps.' She shrugged. 'The harvest will continue until dusk and dinner will not be served until nine this evening.'

'I couldn't . . . '

'*Ma chérie*, you can and you will,' Madame Beaulieu said.

'But what shall I do until then?'

'Whatever you want to do. Enjoy the sunshine.' She cast her eyes upwards. 'While it lasts. The weather reports show that the wind has changed and the storm in the Atlantic is heading this way. We pray it will miss us.'

'I don't want to make him even angrier.'

'Does he care that you are full of remorse?' she asked. 'No! So why should you care if you make him angry?'

Laura grimaced, then decided if she just kept her head down. He would probably not even notice she was there. Thanking Madame Beaulieu for her kindness, Laura ventured outside. She stood for a moment in the garden, trying to catch sight of Philippe, but he was nowhere to be seen. Walking briskly, she headed back to the row of vines where she had left her basket.

Somehow she needed to try and get her brain — and her heart — back on course. She needed to get Philippe Beaulieu right out of her head and start thinking intelligently again, as Laura Kane, journalist.

The afternoon brought a slight change in the weather and she was reminded about the storm that was threatening. Dark clouds appeared over the horizon and a cool breeze sprang up. To Laura's surprise, Madame Beaulieu came from the house, bringing with her one of her own cardigans. She was dressed in cut-off slacks and a smock top. So casual that she looked as if she were going to pick grapes herself.

'A cardigan for you, Laura. It is a little cooler now.' There was an edge to her voice, a sense of urgency in her manner.

'Thank you. Is everything all right, Madame?'

Fear flickered across her face for a second and she looked over at the threatening black clouds. 'The weather forecast is very bad. We hoped the storm would miss the region, but it threatens to come across from the Bay of Biscay. If the wind sends it this way, I dread to think what will happen.'

Laura felt a chill in her blood.

'What will that mean to the harvest?'

'It could mean disaster for all of the growers, not just us,' she murmured, her face pale with anxiety. 'I must find Philippe. *Excusez moi*, Laura.'

Laura watched her hurrying across the lawn towards the grape press building, which she disappeared into.

Laura suddenly felt utterly selfish, feeling so sorry for herself. There was work to be done. If a storm was coming, the sooner the harvest was safely in the better. Her heart lurched. If torrential rain and wind came now, the grapes might be torn from their branches and ruined. A year's work, gone. Philippe would be distraught. All these people who relied on champagne for their livelihood would be ruined. It would be disastrous.

Trying not to think of her own troubles, she got on with her harvesting work, doing her best not to daydream about Philippe. But later that afternoon all her good intentions were swept aside as Philippe stood on a stepladder at the end of the rows of vines, calling for everyone's attention. Laura's heart lurched. He spoke loudly, in French, so that everyone could hear him.

Laura couldn't understand precisely what he was saying, but she got the gist of it. A storm of hurricane proportions was creeping up from the Atlantic. If they were lucky it would miss the Champagne region — if not, the entire crop could be devastated. Not just his vineyards, but throughout the region. Exactly as his mother had said earlier.

A hubbub of anxious voices sprang up. Almost everyone around her made the sign of the cross on their foreheads, lips and heart. Philippe continued his announcement, and she gathered that he was asking everyone to try to work faster because suddenly everyone seemed to have a sense of urgency. The lazy banter amongst pickers ceased and concentration was evident on everyone's faces. Laura did likewise, picking the grapes as fast as she could.

Basket after basket was filled. The large tub at the end of the rows seemed to fill up faster than it could be emptied. People were sweating as they worked. Meal breaks were taken quickly, as everyone hurried to replenish their energies and then get back to work. At one point, as Laura was taking a drink of water, she spotted Philippe in the vineyards, side by side with his workers, picking grapes, filling his basket. Too intent on his work to notice her.

As dusk crept over the vineyards, only a few people stopped working, and Laura guessed they were locals who had to go home to their families. Most people worked on until it was simply too dark to see.

Her head was throbbing when the Frenchman whom she had been working with all afternoon took her basket from her and tapped his wristwatch.

'It is late.'

She forced a smile.

'I'll keep going a little longer.'

'Tomorrow? I see you tomorrow?'

She nodded, but deep down she doubted she would be seeing him or anyone connected with Philippe Beaulieu again. First thing in the morning she would be gone. She had done her best in helping with the harvest. She couldn't stay where she wasn't wanted.

Gradually people gave up as the light diminished and it was impossible to carry on. Laura was hot because of the intensity of the work, but now as she slowed she felt the chill in the breeze and worryingly felt raindrops on her skin. She tried to do more, to finish this last basket and carry it to the press herself.

It was pitch black now, and only the lamps from the marquee and the house cast their glow across the garden. Raymond and some of the others were still working on the grape presses. Raymond took the final basket from her with a grateful smile.

She was tired and cold. The rain was now a heavy drizzle, but blowing in on a strong, unnatural wind, dampening her clothing, making her hair stick like rat's tails to her head.

She made her way back to the house, but as she went to go through the kitchen door, Philippe threw it wide, about to charge out, almost bowling her over.

In the split second that she saw him, Laura saw his expression. He was pale and anxious and he almost fell backwards when he saw her.

'Laura! You are still here!'

'Your mother didn't want me leaving in the state I was in. She's invited me to stay for dinner, but I'll be leaving first thing in the morning so you don't have to worry.'

'You have been grape picking?' He sounded astonished.

'Yes, obviously. It's all hands to the pump, isn't it?'

He continued staring at her, disbelief all over his face.

'But I never expected you to help.'

'I wanted to,' she said softly, loving him so much it was painful.

'I am surprised. I thought that you had left.'

'Sorry to disappoint you.'

'I am already disappointed,' he said, his voice harsh.

She dodged past him, tears stinging her eyes, and ran up the stairs. The man was totally unforgiving. Madame Beaulieu was just coming out of her room as Laura hurried across the landing and Laura asked to be excused from dinner, her appetite gone and the prospect of being in such close proximity to Philippe over dinner, yet so far away emotionally, was unbearable. The older woman, however, would hear nothing of it.

'Dinner is not for another hour. Perhaps your appetite will have returned by then. We are having chicken in white wine. It is a favourite dish of ours.'

'Philippe won't want me sharing it. I'd much rather stay in my room.'

'*Non*! *Ma chérie*, I cannot allow you to go hungry. I'm sure my son's manners will have returned by the time we sit down to eat,' Madam Beaulieu said kindly.

Laura's eyes closed briefly. His manners maybe, but not his mood.

'Would you mind if I went and had a lie down for a little while, Madame?'

'Of course. You are looking so pale,

Laura. I will knock on your door when dinner is ready.'

Attempting a smile, Laura went into her room and showered. Afterwards she lay in her dressing-gown on top of the bed and slept, suddenly exhausted. She awoke when someone tapped her door. She had fallen into such a deep sleep that she was totally disorientated at first. The sound of Madame Beaulieu's voice brought all her misery rushing back.

'Dinner is almost ready, Laura.'

'Thank you. I'll be right down,' she called back, realising now there was no time to think of her appearance. Slipping into a shift dress she ran a comb through her damp hair and went downstairs, guessing she looked as wretched as she felt.

The table lacked the sparkle and finesse of yesterday. Madame Beaulieu was already seated and indicated for Laura to sit opposite her. She reached across and patted Laura's hand.

'Do not look so afraid, Laura. He will not bite you.'

Moments later when Philippe entered, Laura thought he looked like he might just do that. His face was set like stone, his blue eyes were dull, as if a light had gone out in them. He had dressed in a black silk shirt which made him look even more handsome and she wanted to cry out in pain as she looked at him and knew that any love or affection he had for her had died.

'*Bonsoir*,' he said flatly, taking his seat and pouring white wine.

Laura kept her eyes lowered, unable to look into his face, though he barely glanced her way anyway. She was relieved when, a moment later, the cook entered with a tray.

Remembering his manners, Philippe went into his hosting routine, but his tone was flat, his voice controlled, void of any emotion.

'Laura, I hope you like paté, I know you do not have flamboyant tastes.'

'Yes, I do like paté, thank you,' she answered just as stiffly.

They ate the first course in an

agonising silence, and when she sipped her wine she found it dry and unpleasant.

'Try not to pull a face, Laura,' he remarked, glowering at her. 'Mama and I both prefer dry white wine. I can get you some lemonade if you wish.'

She wasn't aware that she'd pulled a face, and guessed he was just taking a dig at her out of spite.

'No, it's fine. Very nice, actually.'

The next course, which was delicious, threatened to be consumed in a similar atmosphere until Madame Beaulieu broke the silence, making conversation about the harvest and whether this year might be a vintage year if the weather held off.

At least Philippe was keen to talk about his champagne, and as mother and son chatted, Laura glimpsed a little of the old Philippe as his passion for his champagne outshone his anger and disapproval of her being there. Once or twice he seemed to forget he was seated at the table with a dreaded journalist and directed some of his conversation her way — and then almost immediately remembered she was the enemy and withdrew again.

Laura did her best to join in the conversation, mainly for Madam Beaulieu's sake. The atmosphere was awful and she was trying so hard to make the evening go smoothly. But Laura felt like they were all walking on egg shells and it could all erupt in accusations at any minute.

When dessert arrived, which Philippe chose not to take, his mother turned the conversation around completely, bringing up the very topic they were all trying so hard to avoid — her job as a journalist.

'This afternoon, Laura, I looked for you on the internet,' Madame Beaulieu began, her eyes lowered as she ate.

Laura shot a glance at Philippe and their eyes met. She was first to look away.

'Did you?'

'*Oui.* I found so many news stories

with your byline on your newspaper's website. I must say, you are an excellent writer. I was most impressed.'

'Thank you,' Laura murmured, wondering why she was bringing this up when they had almost got through the meal without an angry word.

'Your articles seemed so well researched and well composed. There was nothing scandalous or malicious in anything you wrote.'

Laura frowned.

'Why would there be?'

'Indeed. And I was most impressed with your stories relating to that young woman, Lucy Day.'

Laura saw Philippe stiffen and she deliberately avoided looking his way.

'Yes, I imagine you found lots of my stories about her. Her disappearance was headline news for a long while in our town.'

'I did,' the older woman agreed. 'It occurred to me that you went beyond the call of duty to keep her disappearance in the public eye. You made sure people didn't forget about her.'

Laura placed her spoon down and looked at Philippe.

'Believe it or not, I really cared that no-one could find her. I didn't want people to forget. I was just over the moon when I spotted her in that painting of yours, Philippe.'

His eyes locked on to hers for a moment, and this time it was he who turned away first.

'I saw no mention of that in your stories,' Madame Beaulieu remarked.

'No, I didn't write about it. I wanted to try and find out for myself if she really was in the Champagne region or whether she'd vanished from here, too. I wanted to try to find out discreetly.' She looked directly at Philippe then, as she added, 'For all I knew you could have kidnapped her. You could have been holding her against her will.'

'Do I look like that sort of person?' Philippe asked, clearly offended.

'I didn't know you then,' she said.

'And do you know me now?' he

asked, lowering his voice.

'Yes, I think so. At least I thought I did.'

'This is mutual,' he said, his eyes suddenly creasing with pain. 'I thought I knew you, too.' He got up from the table, not looking at either Laura or his mother as he said, 'But the Laura I knew was a figment of my imagination — and your imagination. Laura Stevens, shoe sales lady, does not exist. Would you excuse me?'

The room — and Laura's heart — felt totally empty when he had gone.

A Good Story

Laura offered to help with the dishes, but Madame Beaulieu wouldn't hear of it. There seemed nothing left to do now but retire to her room and pack her things ready to leave first thing in the morning. She informed Philippe's mother of her plans, and the older woman placed the car keys on the coffee table.

As Laura thanked her once more for her kindness and hospitality, Madame Beaulieu caught her arm. She looked incredibly sad.

'It is a pity you are leaving here on such an unhappy note. For a time there . . . ' her voice trailed away and she drew up her slender shoulders and let them fall. 'Ah, *c'est la vie!*'

Laura managed a smile and went to her room. It didn't take long to pack, leaving out just what she needed for tomorrow. She tried to settle down to read a book that she'd brought with her, but concentrating was impossible and after an hour or so of wandering aimlessly about her room, knowing that sleep would be just as impossible, she decided that some fresh air would help. Slipping a cardigan over her thin dress, she went quietly downstairs and out into the garden.

It was still drizzling and the air was even chillier. She was glad of her cardigan as she walked across the lawn. People were settling down in sleeping bags in the marquee, and someone was playing an accordion. She walked past them, acknowledging one or two familiar faces.

Reaching the edge of the vine rows, she stood for a while, taking in the view for the last time. Even though it was dark now and the vines were shrouded in shadow, there was such beauty and serenity about it all. But it was impossible not to dwell on the events of the previous evening, when Philippe had held her close after sketching her.

The ache in her heart told her that she was making it worse for herself by dreaming of the few happy hours she had spent with Philippe. Better to stop thinking, and to try to put it all behind her and forget him. There was no future for her here.

She walked slowly back towards the house, cold raindrops on her face. She halted as she spotted lights on in a downstairs room. The blinds were open and Laura instantly saw that it was Philippe's studio. He was there.

He stood beside a large canvas on an easel, painting. She knew she ought to go straight indoors, but she couldn't. She wanted to gaze at him once more, and so she crept silently across the lawn to the little orchard near to his window. Standing out there in the dark, behind an apple tree, she was invisible to him, while he was in the spotlight, almost as if he were on an illuminated stage with no idea that he had an audience.

Laura knew well enough that she was

encroaching on his privacy, but there was nothing in her heart she could do to stop it. She wanted to look at him, to savour these last few memories of him. It would most likely be the last time she would set eyes on him ever again.

Wrapping her arms around herself as the evening grew chillier, she stood in the darkness, gazing at that beloved face, so lost in concentration as he worked feverishly, stroking paint on to the canvas, lost in the painting, no longer part of the real world.

She wondered what he was working on. The canvas was much larger than the one he had been working on earlier. This was some new work of art, she guessed. She wondered what he would do with all those sketches of her. Would he scrap them? Rip out the pages and tear them into shreds? Most likely, she decided.

Standing there shivering, Laura saw for herself that their wrecked relation-ship certainly hadn't affected his work. It hadn't stopped him painting. She was sure that, if she had to write a newspaper article now, feeling as wretched as she did, she would struggle to string two words together.

The hopelessness of the situation hit her and she realised how ridiculous it was to stand here gaping at him. She needed to go indoors and sleep. She turned and immediately skidded on the wet grass. Her scream was out before she could stop herself. Steadying herself, she ducked back down behind the apple tree. Peeping around the trunk, she saw Philippe peering through his window into the darkness.

She remained hidden for a few moments longer, her hair damp now against her forehead. Glancing at the window again, Philippe was nowhere to be seen, and so she stepped away from cover of the tree — and walked straight into him.

'What are you doing?' he demanded, his words sharp, his eyes dark with suspicion.

'Just getting some fresh air.'

'It's raining!'

'Not much,' she protested.

'Enough to make your hair stick to your head,' he said, looking with disapproval at her appearance. 'What are you doing outside my window?'

Her throat felt horribly dry suddenly. How could she say she was taking one last sorrowful look at the man she had fallen in love with?

'I was just getting some fresh air before going to bed. I didn't think I'd be able to sleep.' That at least was the truth.

'So you were not spying on me?'

She lowered her eyes.

'Well, I could see you, yes, but it wasn't spying.'

His eyebrows arched in disbelief.

'You always walk so close to the trees? I am surprised you didn't trip over a root in the dark. Are you sure you weren't lurking behind a tree and peeping at me through the darkness, out of sight?'

'Absolutely not!' she exclaimed, her

cheeks turning pink.

For a second, she thought she saw the faintest glimmer of a smile on his lips, but he was determined not to crack.

'You look cold.'

'I am a little,' she admitted, aware that the coldness was mainly due to knowing he disliked her so much. 'I was just going in, actually. Early start tomorrow . . . ' Her voice trailed away and she lowered her eyes.

'For you and me both,' he said, stepping away from the tree to stand looking up to the sky. His face was sombre. 'This rain is not good.'

'Will it affect the harvest?'

He glanced her way, his eyebrows arched as if the question surprised him.

'If it gets no worse we will be safe, but the forecast is worrying. There has been torrential rain further to the east.'

She desperately wanted to put her arms around him, to try and take away some of the worry, but it wasn't her place. She had no right.

With a sigh, he turned back to the house.

'Are you coming in? It will do no good just staying outside.'

Laura shivered, realising the cold had seeped through to her skin.

'I am having a brandy. Join me.'

It wasn't a request and Laura knew she had to comply. He led the way into the lounge and she perched uneasily on the edge of the sofa, while he crossed the room to a cabinet and poured two glasses of brandy. Handing her one, and telling her to sip it slowly, he seated himself in an armchair a little distance away. Taking a sip of the warming liquid he sank back into the cushions, eyes closed.

The brandy revived Laura and stopped her from shivering. It also provided her with a little Dutch courage and when, after some minutes, he hadn't said a word, she ventured, 'Philippe, tell me something.'

He opened his eyes and looked steadily at her.

'Off the record, or am I likely to be quoted?'

She gasped. He just wasn't going to let her forget she'd lied about being a journalist. But if that was the way he wanted it.

'Off the record.'

He raised his glass and took another sip.

'Your question?'

'On the night of your exhibition, when I asked you about the girl in the painting, why did you lie? Why did you tell me she was a French student, when you knew full well that she was an English girl who'd run away from home and was hiding out in the next village?'

He barely flinched.

'I knew all that, did I?'

'Well, obviously!' she exclaimed. 'If you'd just told the truth, I wouldn't have been suspicious and been desperate to know more.'

He sat forward in his chair.

'Laura, even if I had known the truth about this girl, I would certainly not

257

have passed details of her private life to a stranger. She obviously had good reason to run away. So, even if I had known her situation, I would not have told you.'

Laura stared down into her glass, realising that what he was saying made sense. Either he had been protecting her, or he actually really didn't know.

'Tell me,' she murmured softly. 'Off the record. Did you know she was a missing person?'

'It may surprise you, but I do not involve myself with every person in the locality. I told you the truth, Laura. When you first asked about her I said I didn't know who she was. You were the one that pressed me for information. I took a guess to satisfy your curiosity. I thought she probably was a student earning a little extra income.'

'So you're saying you didn't know her personally?'

One dark eyebrow shot up and then he frowned.

'You are questioning my honesty?

Have I not just told you that I did not know the girl's background. What exactly are you getting at, Laura?'

'I'm not getting at anything.'

'You are thinking the worst about me, Laura Kane. You people jump to conclusions all the while. Why should it surprise me that you are no different?'

His words hurt her. 'You people' implied she was just another member of the paparazzi, for ever haunting him, when nothing could be further from the truth.

'I'm not like that,' she argued.

'You have just proven that you are,' he replied, his voice becoming dangerously low. 'You are just the same as all those in your profession. And that saddens me beyond belief, Laura. I thought — '

'What? What did you think?' she asked, seeing beyond his anger to a deep sadness that seemed to have enveloped him.

He took another swallow of his brandy, staring down into the glass, saying nothing at first. Then, raising his head, he murmured, 'I thought you and I had something unique, something that we could build upon, see where it led us. But that is impossible and it breaks my heart.'

'And mine, too, Philippe,' she replied, wishing she dared run to him and wrap her arms around him. 'Despite how all this looks, I'm not some hard-nosed journalist who'd sell her granny for a story. I care about people, Philippe. I cared about Lucy Day and the fact that she'd disappeared.'

'But you were here working, following a lead for your story?' he pointed out, leaning forward in his chair.

'Not exactly. My editor wanted me to hand over the information I'd got to the police. He didn't want me getting involved. So I took a week's annual holiday and came over anyway.'

He stared at her.

'So you are not here on official business for your newspaper?'

She shook her head.

He looked surprised, and then his lip curled as if he didn't believe her.

'You say that, but how can I believe your words? You have broken my trust, Laura.'

'I wanted to tell you about my job so many times,' Laura said softly. 'But I'd seen how you reacted to those other reporters. Then when you talked about the media being the scum of the earth and the awful thing that happened to your fiancée, I just never found the right moment to admit what my job was.'

He put his brandy glass down and got to his feet. He crossed to one side of the room and then back again, his expression tight as if he was choosing his words carefully.

'I knew there was something wrong about you, Laura. In all the sketches I made of you, I could never see your true spirit.' He waved his hand in a gesture that implied she wouldn't understand what he meant as he went on. 'There was something elusive about you, some part of you I could not reach. I thought I was losing my touch. But no, it was because you were hiding your real self from me.'

'Only my job, Philippe,' she pleaded, desperately wishing he would take her back into his arms and tell her she was forgiven. 'Everything else you discovered about me was real.'

He turned away.

'No. You are not the person I thought you were. A person's career makes them what they are. In the case of journalists, it is a matter of truth. You seem to have great difficulty in avoiding the lies.'

'That's not fair!' she argued, hurt by his unyielding manner. She was beginning to be thankful that she had seen this other side to him. He was arrogant, self righteous and stubborn. 'I've never written a lie in my entire life. It may come as a surprise to you, Philippe, but I'm as conscientious and passionate about my job as you are about yours.'

He uttered an annoying little laugh and picked up his glass again.

'So you came here just to track down a missing girl. You didn't come to spy on me and sell some piece of fabricated nonsense to the high-paying magazines?'

'Absolutely not! I came to make sure Lucy Day wasn't chained up in your champagne cellars! Because that's what I thought when you told me a pack of lies about her being a student.'

His eyes flashed a look of pure steel.

'You are a journalist. You get paid for your stories. Do you know how many hundreds, even thousands of euros you could earn with a story about me, sold to the right magazines?'

'Oh! Talk about conceited!' she exclaimed, totally infuriated with the man. 'I'm sorry to disappoint you, Philippe, but until I researched that painting and learned who the artist was, I'd never even heard of Philippe Beaulieu. So if you think you're a high-ranking celebrity over here, good for you, but where I come from, you're a total unknown. Sorry to disappoint you!' Placing her glass down, she snatched up the car keys.

'What are you doing?'

'I'm not staying here another minute. I'm leaving!' she snapped.

'Sit down!'

Her anger bubbled.

'Don't tell me what to do!'

He crossed the room in two strides, his hands gripping her upper arms, forcing her back against the cushions. His face was so close to hers she caught her breath, remembering his kiss. As their eyes met Laura thought she saw the anger in his gaze melt, but in the blinking of an eye, the barriers had shot back into place and he straightened, moving away from her.

'You are not leaving now. It's late and it's raining and you need a good night's sleep before driving anywhere.'

'And you need to stop being so self righteous and bossy!' she retaliated, her blood boiling.

For a second his expression softened and the anguish was there again, as it had been on the evening when he told her about his fiancée.

'If you had been through my experiences at the hands of the paparazzi, Laura, then you would understand.'

'I do understand,' she said, her heart melting as she reached out and caught hold of his arm. His sleeves were rolled up and she felt the strength of his tanned forearm as his muscle flexed at her touch.

'I understand how you feel regarding your fiancée. That must have been unbearable, but please don't think we are all like that, dishing the dirt. For the majority we are hardworking, dedicated people committed to reporting the truth, often at great risk to ourselves. Please don't tar us all with the same brush.'

For a moment, he just looked into her eyes and she prayed he would see the truth there. Then his gaze switched to her hand and he pulled free. He crossed to his chair, sat down and took a final gulp of his brandy. For a long while he remained silent and brooding.

Eventually he said, 'I understand you have spoken to the mysterious Lucy Day.'

'Yes. She was here for the grape picking. I saw her name in the ledger.'

'Yes, I did, too,' Philippe interrupted. 'It was on the same page as Laura Stevens.' His expression was glacial. 'So you were keeping up the pretence to the bitter end.'

Laura groaned miserably.

'You know, I considered signing my name as Laura Kane, but then I thought you might see my name before I'd had a chance to tell you.' She looked pleadingly at him. 'I was going to tell you, Philippe. Stupidly, I thought that as we'd got to know one another and seemed to like each other, you wouldn't mind too much what my actual job was. How wrong can you be?'

'Extremely wrong!' he murmured.

'But I am curious. What did the girl have to say when you confronted her?'

'She was shocked and horrified to begin with,' Laura admitted. 'She just ran off. Couldn't get away from me fast enough.' She looked him in the eye. 'A bit like you, really.'

An unkind smile curled his lips.

'You see the power your profession has on people.'

She ignored his remark and continued.

'She was afraid. I went after her and caught her up. I promised her I wouldn't be giving her location away and that her secret life was safe.'

'Indeed!'

Laura saw the look on his face.

'I know you won't believe me, but I gave her my word and I meant it. I won't be telling anyone or writing anything. But I did let her know that the person she was running from is no longer on the scene, and that her mum misses her terribly. I think she will make contact with her mother now.'

He listened, arms folded.

'That is a good story, is it not? The sort of story that sells papers?'

'Absolutely!' Laura agreed. 'But I won't be writing anything. If Lucy wants to broadcast the fact that she's safe, that's up to her, not me.'

Philippe regarded her with suspicion, as if he just couldn't believe a journalist could be trusted with a secret.

'Your editor will not drag the story from you?'

'Wild horses wouldn't. The ball's in Lucy's court now.'

'And you think she will return home?'

Laura shrugged.

'Who knows? She has a boyfriend here who seems to care a lot for her. I personally think she will let her close family know where she is and stop them worrying. But it will be up to Lucy whether she wants to let the papers know. I shan't be saying anything.'

He fell silent for a while again then coldly asked, 'So, Laura, if you do not write the gossip columns, what do you write about in your little newspaper?'

He made her job sound paltry, like it didn't count unless it was splashing the private lives of celebrities all over its pages. Her voice had a raw edge to it as she answered.

'I write about real news. The ups and downs of local businesses, achievements, accidents, crimes, sport, everyday life.'

'And you like your job?'

'I love my job!' she told him fiercely. 'I love the contact with people, I like getting to grips with a story so that I totally understand it, and then I love the challenge of reporting it impartially, so that others can see the truth and make up their own minds. Every day is different. You never know what the next phone call will bring. And it's rewarding, too.' She gazed at Philippe. 'Sometimes it might be something as simple as a lost dog, but by giving the right information, it gets found. It's not just a job, Philippe, it's a way of life. I couldn't do anything else.'

'Well, Laura, well done. You have found something more than a lost dog this time.'

'Yes,' she murmured, giving him a sad smile. He was right; she had found a missing teenager — but lost her heart.

A Happy Man

It was impossible to sleep. Laura tossed and turned in her bed continually, listening to the weather worsening, and wondering and worrying what was happening outside to the vines.

Glancing at her wristwatch, she saw that it was only three a.m., but she knew she wouldn't be able to sleep, not without knowing if Philippe and the vineyard were facing disaster.

She couldn't bear it any longer. She got out of bed and put on her jeans, her warmest sweatshirt and trainers. Delving deep into a side pocket of her suitcase, she found a fold-up plastic raincoat and hood, which she pulled on over everything.

Dressed as best she could for the terrible weather, she went quietly downstairs and out into the night. Rain lashed into her face harshly as she crossed the grass, and tree branches rustled and groaned as the wind bent them out of shape. Within moments of walking across the grass, she started to feel the damp seeping through the canvas of her shoes.

The soft sounds of people sleeping drifted out from the marquee and she was glad for them that the marquee was watertight. Overhead, the sky was a blanket of thick cloud blown angrily across the starless sky.

She walked down towards the vine rows — and then she stopped suddenly. There was someone standing there — a man in a large waterproof cape. He was standing with his back to her, just staring out over the large vineyard, like a statue.

Laura knew at once who it was and her heart lurched. She stopped in her tracks, unsure whether to disturb him. Would he be angry that she was encroaching on his private world? Worse, would he think she was going to write a story about this tragedy?

She didn't know what he would think, and for an eternity she stood there, not sure whether to run back indoors or to approach him.

But as she stood there, he looked so forlorn, so lost and vulnerable. Her heart cried out to him. She loved him, and whether or not he loved her back, she couldn't let him endure this night alone.

She didn't make a conscious decision, but before she knew it her feet were carrying her forwards towards Philippe.

He looked surreal standing there in the darkness, his waterproof looking every inch a cape of long ago as it flapped violently in the wind. She could barely breathe and, as she stepped up to stand closer to him, it was her gasp for breath that made him turn and look at her.

'Laura?'

She didn't look at him. Instead, she stared out across the vines, though there was little to see.

'How are they faring?'

'It is impossible to say. The rain has not eased and the wind seems to be doing its best to blow the fruit right off the branches.'

She nodded and moved just a little closer to his side. She held her breath.

There was nothing to say. All they could do was stand and watch and wait.

Time dragged on, the only sound was the rustling of a million leaves blowing in the wind and the raindrops splattering into the crop and the puddles.

'Are you cold, Laura?' he asked after an interminable silence.

She glanced at him, seeing his face soaked with rain, tiny raindrops glistening on his eyelashes, his mouth shining with rainwater. She couldn't lie to him. He would be able to see her shivering anyway, so she nodded, casting him a small smile at the same time, to assure him she didn't mind.

To her astonishment, he lifted up the base of his cape and invited her to duck underneath it with him. There was a hint of the old humour in his voice when he next spoke.

'I think it was made for an elephant. There is room for two under here.'

She dipped under the outstretched material and found herself pressed close to him, her back to him.

He unzipped the cape at the neck so that she could fit comfortably inside it and, to her delight, his arms reached around her middle, holding her against his flat stomach. Dare she hope?

'We will keep each other warm,' he murmured in her ear.

In the small intimate space, Laura rested against the man she loved. Her head came just below his chin, and his hands had clasped together at her midriff.

Her heart was thudding so furiously she was positive that he'd be able to feel the vibration through her body. But then she realised she could feel his heart beating just as rapidly against her back, and a tiny spark of hope kindled itself somewhere deep within.

Standing together, watching the rain, Laura wasn't sure what to do with her own hands. They had simply hung limply at her sides, but now she needed to move them. She wrapped her arms around his, her hands closing over his. He didn't object and not long after she felt his hand move to gently caress her fingers. The sensation made her heart soar.

Feeling so much drier and warmer, Laura vaguely began to realise that the rain wasn't coming down quite as hard and the wind was losing some of its power. She remained silent, not daring to say anything at first, in case it was just wishful thinking.

There was a faint glow of light in the sky now and she guessed it was growing close to dawn. A pale grey light began to drift across the dark mass of vines, illuminating the land. The rain definitely began to ease off.

She felt a surge of hope rise inside of her.

'Philippe, the rain's stopping. I think

the worst could be over.'

He sounded more cautious and he spoke softly, his breath warm against her skin.

'But we will not be able to assess the damage until dawn. Once it gets a little lighter, then we will know.' He hesitated before adding, 'Laura, thank you for staying with me. This night would have been unbearable if not for you here beside me.'

'Me, a dreaded journalist?'

'You,' he murmured agreeably. 'A beautiful journalist with a beautiful and kind heart.'

Laura's eyes fluttered shut as she heard his words and sensed that he was seeing her in a different light now. She wriggled to turn around in the confines of the cape, until she was facing him. Her arms had nowhere else to go but around his waist. Looking up into his face, she saw the anxiety there, yet it wasn't the total fear she had been expecting to see. There was a glimmer shining in his eyes that wasn't intended for his vines.

'I misjudged you, Laura,' he uttered, looking steadily into her face. 'I insulted and hurt you, yet you are still here for me.'

'Of course I am,' she answered, holding him close, loving him so much she knew that it must be shining from her face. 'Philippe, there's nowhere else I'd rather be than beside you.'

'After my awful behaviour towards you?'

She smiled up at his anxious face.

'Yes, even after your awful behaviour!'

'I apologise. Forgive me, Laura.'

'Of course you're forgiven, I do understand why you dislike my profession, judging by the way the papers have treated you.'

She had no chance to say more. Lowering his head, his lips found hers, and she was lost in the magic of his kiss and her happiness soared.

She had no idea how long their kiss lasted, but when Philippe finally raised his head, a pale silvery sunlight was glinting off the vine leaves. Phillipe eased the waterproof cape over their heads then reached for Laura's hand before he spoke.

'It is time to inspect the damage, Laura. Please come with me — I need you.'

Her eyes filled with tears of joy, and she walked hand in hand with him between the grape vines. Slowly her hopes began to rise. There were no grapes lying battered in the mud as they had feared. They hung in plump green bunches shining with raindrops, not swollen, just looking as they had yesterday, the vine leaves glistening as if they had just been polished.

Philippe saw it, too, and he squeezed her hand softly. His step quickened and they walked briskly from row to row, seeing nothing but lush ripe fruit ready to be picked. After the twentieth row at least, Philippe suddenly picked Laura up and whirled her madly around, laughing with pure joy.

The noise awoke those sleeping in the marquee and, one by one, the pickers wandered out to find that the grapes were there, still intact and life was indeed good. The great news travelled fast and within minutes everyone was up and celebrating.

Laura was locked in Philippe's arms, raising her face to his to receive kiss upon kiss.

'Am I forgiven, Philippe, for not telling you the truth, for hiding my identity?' she asked, anxiously, worried in case this rush of emotion was just in the heat of the moment.

He gazed down at her, his eyes shining with love. He brushed a wet tendril of hair from her brow.

'I am the one who needs forgiveness. I reacted badly. My head went crazy when I learned that the beautiful Laura Stevens, shoe shop girl, did not exist. I thought, so who have I fallen in love with? My head, Laura, it went insane for a while.'

'Did it?' she murmured. 'I thought

you couldn't have cared very much for me, or you'd have been more forgiving.'

'Not cared very much!' He gasped and took her hand again and led her towards the house. 'Come. I have something to show you. Something which I hope will explain to you how much I cared. How much I loved Laura Stevens, shoe girl.'

Puzzled as to what he could possibly intend showing her, she followed him into the house, along the hall and into his studio. He clicked on the lights and she saw the painting standing there on the easel. It was the one he had been working on when she had glimpsed him through the window.

Still holding her hand, he led her closer to the painting and she gasped. Whatever she had expected, it certainly wasn't this.

It was a self portrait. He had painted himself in the vineyard, on his knees, his head bent, grief etched across his face, and in his hand a smashed bunch of grapes and leaves, crushed in his fist.

Just looking at the painting made her want to weep. Never had she seen such misery encapsulated in a piece of art. This was pure grief — utter despair, a heart that was broken.

Laura turned to him, her eyes wide.

'Was this a premonition of the storm and the crop being ruined?'

'Do you see any rain?' he asked simply.

'No,' she said, puzzled. 'The day seems quite bright and sunny.'

'Ah, Laura! The only water is that of my tears.'

'I don't understand,' she murmured, looking from him to the painting and back again.

He gazed over her head at the canvas. His voice was pained as he spoke.

'I began this after I discovered you had lied to me. You were not who you said you were. This, Laura, this is how I felt when I thought I had lost you for ever. When I thought the girl I'd fallen in love with did not even exist. You broke my heart. Nothing mattered — not even the harvest mattered,' Phillipe told her.

'Oh, Philippe!' Laura gasped, turning and burying her face against his chest. 'I didn't know. I never realised I meant this much to you.'

'Well, you did.'

The word rang a hollow bell in the pit of her stomach.

'I'm still here, Philippe. My surname is Kane not Stevens and I write for a living rather than sell shoes, but it's still me. And I love you.'

He shook his head and her heart plummeted. Surely he wasn't still holding a grudge against her, after everything that had just happened. She couldn't bear it.

But then he smiled and stroked her damp hair back from her eyes.

'Ah, *mon chérie*, how I loved my little shoe shop girl, yet I always felt there was something missing, something not quite right. Perhaps that was why I had such trouble trying to capture your image in my sketches. It was because a part of you was hiding from me, Laura. I could not see your true spirit. But now I see you — now I see the real you, and I am head over heels — to coin an English phrase. I am in love. I am a happy man!'

'Oh, Philippe!' Laura murmured, reaching up and kissing him madly. 'And I am a happy woman. Very happy!'

'That is good, and I think that perhaps, when we are married, you will write about my champagne?' He smiled at Laura.

'Married!' She laughed.

'It is too soon?' he asked, looking anxious all over again. 'We will wait until after the harvest, yes? But I think we should at lease raise a toast right now to celebrate our love.'

Filled with love and happiness and hope, Laura's heart soared with joy.

'Yes, that's the least we should do.'

'Champagne!' Philippe rallied.

Teasing him, Laura pulled a face.

'Oh, not that stuff! Haven't you any lemonade?'

Then, giggling madly, she fell into his arms and raised her lips to his.

THE END

We do hope that you have enjoyed reading this large print book.

Did you know that all of our titles are available for purchase?

We publish a wide range of high quality large print books including:
Romances, Mysteries, Classics
General Fiction
Non Fiction and Westerns

Special interest titles available in large print are:
The Little Oxford Dictionary
Music Book, Song Book
Hymn Book, Service Book

Also available from us courtesy of Oxford University Press:
Young Readers' Dictionary
(large print edition)
Young Readers' Thesaurus
(large print edition)

For further information or a free brochure, please contact us at:
Ulverscroft Large Print Books Ltd.,
The Green, Bradgate Road, Anstey,
Leicester, LE7 7FU, England.
Tel: (00 44) **0116 236 4325**
Fax: (00 44) **0116 234 0205**

Other titles in the
Linford Romance Library:

AN UNEXPECTED ENCOUNTER

Fenella Miller

Miss Victoria Marsh has an unexpected encounter in the church with a handsome, but disagreeable, soldier who is recuperating from a grievous leg injury. Major Toby Highcliff believes himself to be a useless cripple, but meeting Victoria changes everything. Will he be able to keep her safe from the evil that stalks the neighbourhood and convince her he is the ideal man for her?

ANOTHER CHANCE

Rena George

School teacher Rowan Fairlie's life is set to change when Clett Drummond and his two young daughters take on the tenancy of Ballinbrae Farm. Clett insists he's come to the Highlands to help the girls recover from their mother's death, but Rowan suspects there's more to it. And why does her growing friendship with the family so infuriate the new laird, Simon Fraser? Is it simple jealousy — or are the two men linked by some terrible mystery from the past?

REBELLIOUS HEARTS

Susan Udy

Journalist Alice Jordan can't believe her misfortune when she literally bumps into entrepreneur Dominic Falconer. She is running a newspaper campaign to prevent him from destroying an ancient wood in his apparently never-ending pursuit of profit. However, when it becomes clear that local opinion is firmly on his side, Alice decides to go it alone. Someone has to stop him and she is more than ready for the battle. The trouble is — so is Dominic.

PASSAGE OF TIME

Janet Thomas

When charismatic Josh Stephens literally blows into her life, Melanie Treloar finds him a disturbing presence in the hostel she runs in west Cornwall. During his job of assessing some old mining remains Josh discovers a sea cave that holds an intriguing secret. When he is caught in a cliff fall — saving Melanie's niece — it is Melanie who comes to his rescue. Although this puts their relationship on a new level, can they solve the many problems that still remain?